DEATH BY GRIT

A Western Adventure

A.T. BUTLER

CHAPTER ONE

Jacob Payne peered at himself in the warped mirror and smoothed down the back of his dark hair. That cowlick was the most unmanageable thing. He frowned, licking his hand to try again.

He was supposed to be meeting Bonnie Loft in less than ten minutes to escort her to church and he wanted to look his best. This would be their first time attending church together; in fact, it would be their first actual outing together since meeting nearly a year ago. He was afraid she might think he was dragging his feet with his courting, but the truth was his jobs and bounties had taken him all over the territory. This Sunday he had finally managed to catch a break.

He tilted his head first to one side, then the

other, trying to see himself as she would. He had washed his face, his neck, and behind his ears. His collar and tie seemed straight. His coat was free of dust. It was just the back of his hair that refused to cooperate.

But Jacob had done his best, and if he fussed at it any longer he was going to be late picking her up. The small, pocket-sized copy of the Bible he had brought with him from Virginia sat on the edge of his washstand. He scooped it up, tucked it away, and headed out the door toward his date.

When Jacob had come west from Virginia nearly nine months ago, he had left most of his life behind. With his wife and infant son dead, and his brothers doing everything they could to drive him away from the family estate, there wasn't much he wanted to remember about his old life. His Bible was an exception. This was the book that he had carried with him into battle, at Manassas and Sharpsburg. It had somehow, miraculously, avoided blood, gunshot, or any other damage. When Jacob filled his saddlebags for the trip west, this pocket edition of the Good Book was one of the first things he had packed.

But now that he was more or less settled in the Arizona Territory, he was ashamed to admit that he had found opportunities to make time for his Bible few and far between. Instead, in his work as a bounty hunter, Jacob found himself on the road most Sundays, away from a church or place of worship. He prayed no matter where he was, of course, but it wasn't the same as the community of a church body. He had taken to leaving his Bible in his boarding house in Tucson. He told himself he was keeping it safe, rather that carting it around the desert.

It wasn't until he had made plans to attend a service with Bonnie Loft that Jacob realized how much he had missed it.

From his boarding house to hers, the walk was only about five minutes. The streets of Tucson were all but empty this early in the morning. Jacob remembered back to the previous weekend; with all the drinking and whoring that went on in this town every Saturday night, it was no surprise that Sunday mornings were quiet as the dead.

On his walk, Jacob passed the coroner's office. Mr. Sylvester had had a busy week. A couple of drunk gamblers had lost their temper and had a shoot-out in the middle of the town. A waste of two good men's potential and all because one had called the other a name. The last Jacob had heard, one of the men was dead and the other suffering from a likely infection; he might have to lose an arm. It was a damned shame. There were a thousand ways one could die on the frontier; killing each other shouldn't be one of them.

At that thought, Jacob climbed the front steps to Bonnie's boarding house. The front porch held several wooden chairs, welcoming visitors and giving the landlady a throne from which to hold court on her weekdays. Jacob wondered if he would be invited to sit on this porch with Bonnie one evening.

Maybe if you start courting her properly, he chided himself.

His knock on the door was answered almost immediately by Mrs. Withers, Bonnie's landlady. Her scowl told Jacob all he needed to know about his chances.

"Mr. Payne," she said coldly. She wore a floral apron over a fine Sunday gown, and her ashy-brown hair was pulled back in a tight bun. Clearly she wanted to return to whatever he had interrupted.

"Good morning, Mrs. Withers," he said, removing his hat. "I've come to collect Miss Loft for church."

"Oh, you've decided to start going to

church, have ya? Now that a pretty girl will go with ya?"

"What? No, I—"

"Save it," she said, holding up her hand to stop him. "You men are all alike, all guns blazing, looking to hook any pretty face you can."

Jacob kept his mouth shut; interrupting her would not improve the situation. He had withstood worse insults.

"You think you can kill men for money and then just absolve all your sins by going to church once?"

When he was certain she'd said her piece, he bowed his head and said, "No, ma'am, I—"

But the old woman wasn't done. "Oh, you don't fool me—"

"Thank you, Mrs. Withers," a voice nearly shouted from deeper inside the house, interrupting the older woman's tirade. The door opened wider and Bonnie smiled apologetically at Jacob. "Thank you. We'll be going now. I'll be home later."

"You best come right home, Miss Loft. Don't let this vagabond talk you into a Sunday afternoon drive or any canoodling."

"Thank you!" Bonnie waved at her landlady over her shoulder as she practically dragged Jacob back down the porch steps, away from the house. "I'm so sorry," she said in a lower voice as they reached the road.

"She doesn't much like me, does she?" Jacob teased.

They continued down the street, arm in arm, walking companionably to the nondenominational church Bonnie had been attending since she got to town. Their path took them past the Mission San Xavier del Bac. They walked through the shadow of that Catholic church, where most of the Latino and Irish citizens of Tucson were pouring in.

"Thank you for coming to church with me this morning, Jacob," Bonnie said. "I'm so sorry Mrs. Withers was so rude to you."

"She's not that much different from most folks," he said with a shrug. "She thinks I kill men for money."

"Well . . ." Bonnie blushed. "I did tell her you're a bounty hunter. Many of those posters say 'dead or alive' . . . I guess she just assumed."

"Bonnie," he said quietly, "you know I don't do that, right?"

"I know."

"I've never yet had to kill a man. Every single bounty I've collected has been after capturing the wanted outlaw. Every one."

"I know," she said again, more gently this

time. "But you have to know how rare that is, Jacob. Mrs. Withers believes what she does because of all the other bounty hunters she has heard of. They set quite the bloody example."

Jacob sighed. They had reached the door of the Everlasting Hope Church, a small, white wooden structure built on the outskirts of town where empty streets stretched into the desert. Men who claimed to know said that neighborhoods would be built out this way as the town grew, but Jacob had yet to see any evidence of that.

The man Jacob knew must be Pastor Ambrose was at the door, shaking hands and greeting each member of his flock who came to worship that day. Bonnie only had positive things to say about her pastor, and Jacob had heard all of them. About how this young Pennsylvanian had built church communities all through the states and now into the territories. About how he forswore a salary beyond his bare necessities. About how his wife and small children waited in St. Louis for him to bring them out. From all Jacob had heard, Pastor Ambrose was a man to admire.

"Miss Loft," he said warmly, taking her small hand in his. "How lovely to see you, my dear.

Your presence at Everlasting Hope is always treasured. And who is your friend?"

"Jacob Payne, sir." The two men shook hands. "Thank you for having me."

"Of course, Mr. Payne." The pastor's eyes twinkled as he took in the other man. "Everyone is welcome here. Thank you for coming."

As the pastor turned to greet the next congregant walking up the path, Bonnie touched Jacob's arm lightly, getting his attention.

"Let's find seats."

The chapel was already more than half full; Jacob followed Bonnie's lead to take seats in the middle of a row near the back. As they got settled, Jacob looked around the church. Two large windows on either side of the altar let light stream into the chapel. On the pulpit sat one small floral arrangement, adding a splash of color in the otherwise modest white room. All around them, Tucson locals greeted one another, wishing each other good morning and inquiring about the other's week.

Jacob sighed contentedly. He had missed the welcoming comfort of being part of a congrega-tion. He spent the whole of the prayers, songs, and sermon with a slight smile on his face, wondering why he hadn't made time for this before now.

After church, Bonnie took his arm again and they strolled slowly together through the town.

"What did you think?" Bonnie asked. "I just love Pastor Ambrose. His sermons always seem to be exactly what I need to hear."

Jacob nodded, smiling. "I enjoyed it. Thank you for inviting me. I needed that more than I realized."

Bonnie smiled up at him and squeezed his arm affectionately. "You're invited to join me at church any time, Jacob. I'd love to be able to share this with you."

Jacob heard the intimate tone in her voice and his heart skipped a beat. This wholesome, beautiful woman was always making him feel wanted and better than he deserved. Being with Bonnie was such a stark contrast to constantly chasing after cruel, dirty, conniving outlaws. He could so easily get used to this. Maybe even enough to make him want to stop hitting the road altogether.

"We told Mrs. Withers that I would bring you straight home after church," Jacob said softly.

"Yes, that's true."

Jacob thought he heard a note of disappointment in her voice.

"But," he continued, "I would love to see you tomorrow, if that's acceptable. Either before or after you go to work at the cafe?"

They had reached the path leading to her boarding house. Bonnie turned to face him. "I would love that."

"Good." Jacob grinned. "Great. I'll, um . . . I'll come back here for you tomorrow morning, then?"

"Yes, please. Thank you." The enormous smile on her face mirrored his own.

"My pleasure."

He leaned down, kissed her cheek, and watched as she walked up the steps and into her boarding house.

Jacob couldn't wait for tomorrow.

CHAPTER TWO

"You again?" Mrs. Withers asked when she opened the door to Jacob on Monday, not long before lunchtime. "What do you want?"

Jacob removed his hat. "Good morning, ma'am. Is Miss Loft at home?"

The harsh smell of vinegar met Jacob's nose. Mondays must be cleaning days for Mrs. Withers, which meant he was unlikely to be invited inside. Jacob was glad he had already made plans to take Bonnie out—out of the house and away from her landlady's disapproving eye.

Mrs. Withers sniffed. "Maybe. Maybe not. I don't know that she'll want to see you. She's a good girl. She doesn't need to be spending time with a man like you."

Jacob bit back a retort and looked at his feet

before answering. "I believe Miss Loft is expecting me, ma'am. Could you tell her I'm here, please?"

She shot him one more scowl before closing the door in his face.

Jacob was at a loss. Was Mrs. Withers going to fetch Bonnie or was she simply shutting him out? Should he wait? He replaced his hat on his head—covering that tenacious cowlick—and turned to look out at the street. Without spending the day with Bonnie as he had intended—had been looking forward to, even— Jacob didn't know how he would fill his day.

While he was still considering his options, the door behind him opened again and Bonnie exited onto the porch. Although the details and intricacies of women's fashion were beyond him, Jacob couldn't help but appreciate how her alabaster skin looked against the dark purple of her gown. He almost couldn't take his eyes off the way her tiny waist was set against the wide bell of her skirt.

Simply put, Bonnie Loft took his breath away.

Though she seemed happy to see him, her tight smile hinted at how she'd had to deal with Mrs. Withers. The older woman was protective, there was no doubt about that. At least Jacob could relax in knowing Bonnie would be safe whenever he had to leave town for a job.

"She let you out?" he teased. "Unchained your bonds?"

"Barely." She relaxed into a relieved smile. "Let's hurry, though. Before she tries to stop me again."

He offered his arm and led her down to the road and toward the center of town.

"I thought we could take in a picnic lunch," he suggested cautiously.

"A picnic? As in . . . eating outside?" She looked confused and startled at the very suggestion.

He couldn't read her expression, so he plowed ahead with his explanation. "I know if we were somewhere other than the lawless territories we wouldn't be able to see each other without a chaperone and formal calling. So, I was thinking that instead we could enjoy the gorgeous day. I know eating outside might seem strange or even uncouth to you, but it's something I do all the time. It's not as bad as it sounds. One of the perks of the job, sometimes."

"That sounds . . . nice," she said slowly. "I don't know how to do that. You'll show me?"

"Of course. Trust me."

He led the way to San Xavier Cafe. Earlier that morning, he had already talked to Mickey and Mrs. Everill about his plan. Everything should be ready and waiting for them, all the supplies they would need for their lunch outside.

Jacob hadn't had a chance yet to really talk to Bonnie about her past, about where she came from before arriving in the territory. But the idea of a picnic in the middle of the day was something he missed from his life in Virginia. It had been too hot in Tucson most of his time here so far, but now, as the fall season began, he could better enjoy it. And he couldn't wait to share it with her.

It was a bit of a walk, but at the foot of the small peak near town, Jacob found a lovely green area for them to sit and relax. He spread out the blanket on the ground, laughed at Bonnie's confused expression, and helped her situate herself. Sitting was a bit of a balancing act in that gown, but she seemed eager to try.

Jacob withdrew their meal from the basket Mrs. Everill had packed and proudly served Bonnie lunch, after so many times of her doing the same for him.

Not long after they began, Jacob was distracted by movement. He never could relax.

Given the demands of his job, he always felt as though he were on guard for something. Out of the corner of his eye, Jacob saw Tucson's U.S. Marshal, Owen Santos, approaching. As soon as he realized the marshal was headed toward him, Jacob stood to greet him.

"Mr. Santos." He shook the man's hand. "What can I do for you?"

Santos glanced at Bonnie, tipping his hat in greeting, though he seemed distracted. "Payne. There's not much time. I need you on the trail. Now. As soon as possible."

Jacob's stomach dropped. All this effort he had put in for this one small window of time with Bonnie, and now the law was asking him to abandon it. But, Jacob knew, this was the job. Santos had plenty of his own deputies to boss around; he wouldn't be asking the bounty hunter unless the situation was dire.

"What is it?"

Bonnie stayed quiet, watching the conversation between the two men. Santos caught her eye and his face flushed slightly. Jacob didn't miss a thing.

"Should we head to your office?" he suggested.

"Yeah." Santos looked at Jacob again,

nodding vigorously. "Yes. My office. I can fill you in there."

"All right. Give me a few minutes to walk Miss Loft home, and I'll be right there."

Though Santos seemed reluctant to let even that much time pass, he gave one last curt nod and quickly strode away. Whatever this pressing bounty was, it had the lawman worried; Jacob could read the anxiety in every twitch of the man's muscles. Jacob began to mentally catalog what he would need to pack, depending on how far Santos was sending him.

"I'm so sorry, Bonnie," Jacob said, turning to his companion. "I had hoped we would at least have been able to finish lunch."

"I know. Me too." She smiled sadly. "Maybe when you get back?"

They packed up the remains of the lunch. Bonnie folded the blanket and tucked it under her arm. Jacob offered his arm to her once again, wondering when their next window of time might appear.

After walking in silence for a couple blocks, Bonnie spoke up. "Do you enjoy being a bounty hunter?"

He answered immediately; there was no question. "I do. It's rarely easy, but it's work that needs to be done."

"And you're good at it," she prompted.

"I am." Jacob was not one to boast, but he knew his strengths. "There are not many men can bring in an outlaw without resorting to killing them. I know the reputation bounty hunters have. I know what most people expect of us. But if I can make a difference in just a few lives by doing this job efficiently and safely, I can be proud of my work."

"I'm proud of you too, Jacob."

They had reached her front porch, and Jacob was loath to leave her. This new bounty could take him away from Tucson for days, if not weeks. At the very least he'd likely have to miss church with her next Sunday.

But when he looked into her eyes, he knew she'd wait for him. Without saying a word, with just that expression of faith and pride, she beamed at him. Her contented smile communicated her loyalty and steadfastness to the man standing before her. It didn't matter how long he had to be gone, doing his duty and ridding the Arizona Territory of dangerous men. She would look for him every day until he came home.

"Take care of yourself," he said. "I'll see you soon, Miss Loft."

Her smile turned tender. "Mr. Payne."

She turned and was inside.

As he made his way to the U.S. Marshal's office, Jacob tried to shake the feel of Bonnie next to him, the scent of her. He needed pure focus to catch his next outlaw, and she wouldn't want him to be distracted.

"Finally!" Santos said under his breath as Jacob entered. "We have a lead, but it could already be cold. Can you be ready to go within the hour?"

"Of course. What do I need?"

Santos handed him the bulletin with the criminal's picture and details. He'd be looking for an Irishman, approximately in his forties and shorter than six foot. The bounty for murderer and thief Seamus Maloney was one thousand dollars, the largest Jacob had ever pursued. He studied the face he would be looking for: thin blond and gray hair, cropped close to his head; a wide, sweeping blond and gray mustache and goatee; long, thin nose that looked as though it had been broken at least once; and gray-blue eyes, glaring at him.

"Maloney is one of the Slippery Stone Gang. We think he's on his own, either because Stone threw him out or because he left of his own accord, who knows. Point is, he'll be smart and he'll be prepared. He's sure to know there's a bounty on his head already."

"Says here he murdered seven people? Can that be right?" It took a hard man to murder so many people, let alone get away afterward. Jacob had never come across such a man.

Santos nodded. "He held up a stagecoach and killed everyone on board. Or tried to. One of the passengers played dead and got away, though I understand he's still recovering from the gunshot and it isn't certain he'll make it. Which could bring the death toll to eight."

"Damn," Jacob said under his breath. That was cold-blooded for anyone to do, let alone one man working on his own. "All right. What's the lead?"

"I just got a wire from Haven."

"West of here?"

"That's right. The sheriff has his hands full with some local land dispute and just a single deputy to back him up. It was the schoolteacher who sent the wire, if you can believe it. She thinks Maloney is holed up in town there under the name Moore."

"How sure is she?"

"Hard to tell from the wire, but sure enough to send it. Sure enough that I want you out there. Now, if possible."

"All right. I'll go. I'll wire you news from Haven."

"You're a good man, Jacob." Santos shook his hand. "I don't know what you're bound to find in Haven, but be careful."

"I always am."

There was a sudden twinkle in the other man's eye. "Seems like you've got something good to come home to, leastways."

Jacob smiled. "Yes, sir. Thank you."

As he walked away from the marshal's office, Jacob wondered if the bartender, Mickey, would be pleased to see him again. Returning the blanket and basket from his picnic, only to insist on another lunch to be packed up even more quickly.

Less than an hour later, Jacob was packed with his trusty horse Blaze on the road to Haven.

CHAPTER THREE

Afternoon was without a doubt the worst time to be out under the sun, riding into the desert west of Tucson. At least it was October, not the summer, Jacob reflected. But he needed to get to Haven before sunset, so he couldn't wait for the cooler part of the day. The sooner he got there, the sooner the schoolteacher and all the other citizens could be made safer. If Maloney could murder a full stagecoach full of people, being on the run and in the middle of a small town wasn't any guarantee he would lay low.

The road to Haven was familiar to Jacob; other bounty hunts had taken him in this direction. With Blaze comfortably following the road, Jacob could let his thoughts wander back to his morning with Bonnie and the previous day's visit to Everlasting Hope Church.

Such thoughts inevitably led to Jacob thinking about the last time he had been in a place of worship—the Goose Creek Church in Charlottesville, Virginia. Goose Creek Church had been his home church all through his childhood and into young adulthood. His family's estate had only been six miles away; he grew up attending services in that small clapboard building every Sunday with his parents and three brothers.

Jacob had loved that church, loved the community of neighbors he was a part of for so much of his life. His first love—when he was eight years old—he met at that church. His first understanding of right and wrong, his first reflection on death. His wedding had been held at Goose Creek Church, as well as his wife and son's funeral. The church was almost as much a part of him as his family's plantation had been.

But it was a conflict in that very building that had led to Jacob fleeing the eastern United States and finding his way to Tucson, Arizona.

His younger brother Jackson had started some project on the family plantation. Even now, Jacob couldn't remember all the details, even though this had been the cause of the family disagreement that had driven him west. A new building or a subdivided field. Something not important in the long run, but which at the time had had a monumental effect on his life. Jacob's other brothers, James and John, hadn't put up a fight, just gone along with what Jackson had wanted. Jacob was on his own.

Though Jacob was the oldest, their father Joseph had long ago turned over control of the plantation to Jackson. He was never quite sure why his father had overlooked him like that. Jacob was sure that any blunders of his youth had been long forgotten. But every time he tried to bring up the conversation with his father, he was ignored or shut down. For some unknown reason his father saw Jackson as the better choice, and nothing Jacob did could change that.

Jacob's wife and son had been dead only a few years, and he had come back to the family estate ostensibly to help take care of their parents and lend help to his brothers while he tried to find his way again. But at every turn, Jackson belittled and demeaned him. He'd assumed Jacob had nothing else to do other than attend to his assignments; the oldest brother, after all, had given up his say over the estate.

Finally, Jacob had had enough.

This particular Sunday morning—his last one there—as Jacob escorted their mother to the family pew, Jackson began chattering at him again. Even though it was Sunday, and they were literally in church about to begin the service, he had launched into the list of things he needed Jacob to do the following week.

Jacob kept his calm long enough to see his mother settled and then turned to face Jackson. The other man was much closer than Jacob had realized, and in his surprise and anger, Jacob hauled back and punched his brother square in the nose right in the center aisle of the Goose Creek Church.

Jackson bled all over the front of his suit, yelling out and delaying the church service for hours while things settled down.

But Jacob was gone before that happened. A short trip home to gather his most treasured possessions, and then he was heading west. He had felt stuck. He had no other prospects in Virginia, no other property, and it seemed as though his family expected him to give up his claim to this property. He wouldn't stay one more day under his younger brother's thumb.

Jacob could admit now that he left Virginia in a fit of temper. That may not have been the best circumstances under which to make a life-altering decision, but now that he was in Tucson, he was pleased. This new life was where he was supposed to be; he was sure of it.

But that was all in the past now. Jacob could fantasize about saving up enough money, riding back to Virginia, and thrusting a sack of money at Jackson to buy the family home right out from under him. But would he really do that? Would he want to leave the freedom of the western territories?

He was beginning to realize that any decision he made about his future would need to start with the consideration of what Bonnie might want as well. Not yet, of course—it was far too soon for him to be asking her to marry him. But if things kept progressing, it would be a step in the future. The first thing he needed to do was gain her permission to court her in earnest.

Thinking about future outings and conversations with Bonnie was enough to keep his mind busy for the final miles of his trip.

After another hour, the town of Haven appeared on the horizon in front of him, the flat desert stretching for miles in each direction. Saguaro cacti peppered the landscape, and as Jacob drew nearer to the town he noticed a few mesquite trees here and there. Haven was a tiny town, founded only five or so years earlier. It was big enough to host a one-room schoolhouse and jail, but not a hotel. It seemed a strange place for an outlaw to head, given that there were likely few newcomers, but maybe Maloney had a bigger plan.

Jacob rode slowly into town, the citizens of Haven nodding at him in greeting. Not a single person seemed the least bit concerned about the presence of a murderer in their town. He found the sheriff's office dark and locked, and after asking a passing couple for directions, made his way to the schoolhouse.

CHAPTER FOUR

Haven's one-room schoolhouse was impossible to miss as Jacob rode through the small town. Near the end of the main road, close to where the first houses had sprung up, the schoolhouse was the only building on the street that boasted any color whatsoever. Where the other buildings existed only in shades of brown and beige, the schoolhouse drew attention to itself with bright red shutters and front door.

Jacob smiled to himself to think about what it must be like to be a child in this town.

He dismounted and approached the building. The door stood ajar. As it was after school hours, all the students were gone for the day, but a woman stood with her back to the door as she cleaned off the chalkboard. She didn't seem any older than Jacob, though she boasted jet-black hair where his own was starting to gray.

Jacob knocked lightly on the door. She looked up, a puzzled expression crossing her face.

"Can I help you?"

"Yes, Miss . . . ?"

"Mrs. Larson."

"Mrs. Larson. My name is Jacob Payne. The U.S. Marshal in Tucson received your telegram and sent me to see about your safety."

Her puzzlement turned to a frown. "*My* safety?"

"The town's, ma'am. So to speak. Can I ask you some questions?"

She wiped chalk off of her hands onto her apron. "Heavens, yes. Why don't you come and have dinner with my husband and me at our home and we can talk it over?"

"With all due respect, ma'am, if the wanted man in question is who you think it is, I think it's best I get the details as soon as possible."

"Oh, of course. You're right. I'm sorry. I don't know what I was thinking. I'm not used to this."

"That's all right, ma'am. Is it okay with you if I sit down?" Jacob gestured to the last row of desks in the schoolhouse. It'd be a tight fit for him, but might make her feel more comfortable.

"Yes. I'm sorry. I should have offered. I'm just so flustered."

Jacob sat, nodding in understanding. "Let's start at the beginning. You saw a man you believe to be the murderer Seamus Maloney, correct?"

"I did."

"And this man—I believe the telegram said he's using the name Moore. When did you first see him?"

Mrs. Larson stood at the head of the school-room and wrung her hands, though she spoke loudly and confidently as though she were teaching her class. "Just this morning, before school. The children and I were out in the yard when he rode by on a dark horse—almost black, it was. I wouldn't have thought anything of it, but the look he gave me . . ." She clutched her hand to her bosom. "Mr. Payne, there is nothing more frightening than the way an uncouth man can look at a defenseless woman."

"I can imagine, Mrs. Larson. That must have been difficult. How did you know who it was?"

"My husband is the deputy here. Haven may

be a small town, but we get a certain level of knowledge about the law enforcement."

"Of course," he said, discomfited. "I didn't mean to imply otherwise."

She inclined her head, acknowledging his apology. "So, of course, I have seen the man's wanted poster. It was Seamus Maloney. I have no doubt. The same cold blue eyes, the same gray-blond mustache."

"And did you see where he went after he rode past?"

"Oh, heavens, no." She shook her head, flustered. "No. Certainly not."

Jacob was unclear why she seemed so offended by his question. "My apologies. I didn't mean to imply . . . anything."

"I gathered the children and came right back inside. I wanted nothing further to do with him."

"But—" Jacob was confused. "You sent a telegram, didn't you?"

She sighed. "Not exactly."

"Wait." He put his hand up, pausing to gather his thoughts and figure out how to word his next question. "Can we start earlier, then? Who sent the telegram to the marshal's office?"

"That was my husband. The deputy. I told you about him."

"So you saw Maloney, told your husband about it, and then *he* sent the telegram?"

"Apparently." She sighed. "He didn't tell me he was going to, though. Your appearance here is quite the surprise to me."

Jacob's mind was whirring. Why would a deputy hide the fact he sent a telegram?

"On second thought, Mrs. Larson, could I possibly take you up on your offer to have dinner with you and your husband? I may have spoken too hastily earlier. I didn't realize he had any part in this."

"Yes. Please. Yes. Let's do that." Mrs. Larson's shoulders relaxed, and she seemed relieved. "I only have one more chore to take care of here and then we can walk back to my home."

With a couple quick instructions, Mrs. Larson had Jacob moving stacks of primers and between the two of them managed to finish and lock up the schoolhouse in no time. When they exited the building together, Mrs. Larson looked at the sky and sighed.

"Truth be told, Mr. Payne, with the days getting shorter like this and the sun setting so early, I'm quite grateful to you for showing up here like you did. I usually don't mind walking home alone—it's not far. But today I'm just rattled."

"I understand completely."

She led the way down the path, through the gate, and turned right onto the main road of Haven. Plenty of citizens still walked the streets, and every single one stopped Mrs. Larson to say hello and not-very-subtly inquire who the stranger was. More than one woman expressed relief that a man of his authority was in the town. Jacob was gratified, making no promises but doing his best to reassure each of them of his goals.

The town livery happened to be on their way, so Jacob could stable Blaze for the evening. With all the interruptions, it took them nearly thirty minutes to walk the half mile to the Larsons' home. The sun had just about set on the flat desert horizon, and the lamps within the house were already lit when they entered.

"Oh, Grover must already be home!" Jacob's companion said cheerfully. "We're lucky his official duties let him stay close to home so often."

She let them in, called hello to her husband, and offered to take Jacob's coat and hat. The bounty hunter found himself standing in the main room of a simple home. There were two wooden chairs positioned at a large wooden table near the front door, with a kitchen and doorway to another room near the back.

A portly man with a thick brown beard came striding across the room to greet him, hand outstretched to shake.

"Howdy, Mister . . . ?"

"Payne." He shook Mr. Larson's hand. "Jacob Payne. Sent here by the marshal in Tucson after he got your wife's telegram."

"Oh, yes. Marvelous."

"Although I understand from her that you are the one who actually sent it?"

"That's right, that's right. Here, why don't you have a seat? We still have a bit to wait while my wife makes supper."

Jacob looked to the kitchen, where Mrs. Larson had already donned an apron and begun to scrub vegetables clean. God bless women of the frontier who were called upon to do so much for their home and household, he thought. Jacob had a flash of memory of his sister-in-law, Jackson's wife, whom he had never seen wear an apron in her entire life. First the unpaid laborers of her childhood then the paid help after the war had taken care of all the things that women like Mrs. Larson handled themselves here in the Arizona Territory.

Jacob took a seat at the kitchen table,

wondering where Maloney was at that moment. How far away he was getting while the kind people of Haven stalled him with hospitality.

"Mr. Larson, can we get down to it? Did you see Maloney at all?"

"Me? Oh, no. No, no, no. No, I didn't. I merely relayed what my wife told me."

"Have you heard any other reports of him in Haven? Any other citizens coming to you with stories or concerns?"

"Well, now, let me think."

Larson leaned back in his chair, and hooked his thumbs into his belt just below his round stomach. Jacob had a quick, uncharitable thought that a man as out of shape as Deputy Larson would not be the kind of man Jacob would want pursuing an outlaw with him, but put it quickly from his mind. He didn't even know what his next step should be. Maybe Larson could be helpful.

"Now that you ask, I do think there might have been hints of Maloney around town for a couple days."

"A couple days?" Jacob repeated, shocked. "You say he's been in Haven since his crime and no one has reported it or apprehended him? How is that possible?"

"It's as I say, Mr. Payne." Larson frowned. "I think there might have been hints. I could be wrong, or maybe the hints were wrong, or . . ." He shrugged. "I'm no expert."

Jacob's mouth fell open in surprise, though he closed it quickly. He weighed his next words, keeping in mind he was speaking to both his host and a man of the law who technically had more authority than he did.

"Well, Mr. Larson, did you follow up on any of those hints? Did the sheriff here?"

"Sheriff Whitaker? You know, I'm not sure. He's been awfully busy with that land dispute this week, so he might not of got to it."

Jacob could not believe what he was hearing. He tried to stay calm and start over again at the beginning.

"All right, well, I suppose that's understandable. But seeing as the marshal sent me here to do what I could to capture this murderer, any information you or anyone else in Haven can give me would be useful. I'd appreciate it if you could tell me everything you know."

Deputy Larson spent the next thirty minutes talking in circles and giving vague allusions and theories as he reported what had happened in Haven over the previous forty-eight hours. Mrs. Larson finished up her cooking and served the two men as Jacob lost the last bit of his patience. So far this trip had yielded nothing useful except for the fact that Maloney was probably seen in town that morning.

As they began to eat the sausage and fried potatoes that Mrs. Larson had prepared, Jacob decided to change the subject. He would try again in the morning with the sources they'd pointed him to. He reminded himself to show gratitude for their hospitality.

"This meal is just perfection," he said to his hostess. "I can't thank you enough for welcoming me into your home and helping me out the way you have."

Mrs. Larson smiled and offered him another biscuit. "It's nothing, Mr. Payne."

"There is one other thing you can help me with, if you don't mind?"

"What's that?" Deputy Larson said through a mouthful of food.

"Could you point me in the direction of a hotel or boarding house where I might stay tonight?"

The Larsons looked at each other, communicating wordlessly in the way only married couples can.

"Oh, Mr. Payne," she began, "I'm so sorry. Haven doesn't have a hotel. This isn't the kind of town people visit."

That surprised Jacob. The town was big enough for a school, after all. She must have spoken true when she said that families came here to live, not to pass through.

"What about a boarding house or . . . is there any free bed I could acquire?"

"Well . . . there *is* one place," Deputy Larson said hesitatingly.

"I'd be grateful."

"You won't like it."

Jacob bit back an angry reply. "That may be, sir, but I'm not sure I have a choice."

"Well . . . as far as I know, the cell in the jail is empty. There's a cot there. We can set you up with an extra blanket."

Jacob stared at the deputy, unsure if he was being serious. "You want to lock me up?"

"No, sir. No, no, no, absolutely not. No, I'd leave the cell unlocked for you, of course. You'd just be using it as a place to sleep."

Jacob took another bite of his potatoes so he could think and avoid answering right away. He wasn't sure he had any other options, and it was better than sleeping outside, if just barely.

He nodded. "That sounds like a workable solution."

"Wonderful!" Larson exclaimed. "I'll take you over after supper."

"That'd be perfect," Jacob said, already eager to leave.

CHAPTER FIVE

Jacob had had a long day of riding. He couldn't believe that just that morning he had been knocking on Bonnie's door. So much had happened since then. Though he had never before had to sleep in a jail cell, he found that he was tired enough that the awkwardness of the situation didn't bother him. The extra quilt from the Larsons proved necessary, but he quickly fell asleep on the narrow cot in the tiny cell.

After a few hours of solid sleep, though, Jacob slept fitfully. The uncertainty of what his next step was weighed on him, distracted him. He couldn't feel secure in his duty as he didn't feel secure in his information. As the night wore on, Jacob's mind spun with all the things he would need to remember to do the following day. He had so many loose threads to attend to. Eventually, not long before dawn, Jacob finally drifted off to sleep. He would just have to make do with a few hours. Once Seamus Maloney was taken into custody he could sleep again.

But even those brief, restless hours were cut short when Jacob was brought rudely to consciousness with the muzzle of a gun jabbed into his neck.

"Who the hell are you?" an angry male voice asked.

Jacob's eyes flew open but he didn't dare move. It took him a moment for him to remember where he was and what he was doing there. Evidently whoever had come across him didn't have that information.

"Who are you, I said!"

"Jacob Payne. Bounty hunter. Deputy Larson offered me this bed to sleep in while I'm in town."

"Oh, he did, did he?"

The questioning man backed up a step, but kept his gun trained on Jacob. He was older than Jacob by several decades, fully gray on top and as overweight as Larson. The bounty hunter sat up in the jail cot slowly, not wanting to make any sudden moves or spook the man in any way. Now that he was fully awake, he realized two things. First, that he had taken off his holster and weapon, and the other man now held it clenched tightly in his grip. And second, that the other man wore a sheriff's badge proudly on his chest.

"Are you Sheriff Whitaker by chance?"

"Course I am. Who else would find you in the jail at seven o'clock in the morning?"

"And," Jacob sighed, "am I correct in assuming that your deputy didn't send word or leave a note at all about my presence here?"

"No, he didn't. He'll probably come in and process your arrest warrant later today, though. Might as well tell me what you've done to land yourself in here before then."

Jacob shook his head. "Sorry, sir, I haven't committed any crime. I told you. The deputy offered me a place to sleep."

"Sure." The sheriff laughed derisively. "Sure he did. So you were probably drunk out of your gourd, then, huh? Don't remember being brought in here?"

"I remember perfectly well," Jacob said. He was trying to remain calm, and kept his hands flat on his knees where the sheriff could see them at all times. "This was in lieu of Haven having a hotel of any kind."

"All right, buddy. Fine then. Don't tell me."

"Sheriff. Please. What can I tell you to get you to believe me? I don't have all day to sit in here."

The sheriff outright guffawed. "I don't know where you think you're going instead," he said as he walked out of Jacob's cell.

Jacob stood, but saw immediately it was pointless. The sheriff closed the cell door, locked it and stowed the key.

"If you're not going to talk, we'll just wait 'til Deputy Larson reports in," he said with a shrug. "No skin off my back."

"Is there nothing I can say?" Jacob protested. "Didn't you see for yourself that my weapon was still in here with me? Would the deputy have allowed that if I was arrested for some crime?"

"Between you and me, yes. He might have."

Jacob groaned in frustration.

"Don't worry, Payne," the sheriff said as he walked away. "You'll get your meals same as any other prisoner, even if you are getting on my last nerve."

The hallway from the cell was short, and Jacob watched the sheriff the whole way back to the front office. He turned the corner at the last moment to go to his desk, and out of

Jacob's sight, but he knew he would still hear him.

"Sheriff Whitaker, please. Telegraph the marshal in Tucson. I swear I have done nothing wrong and wasn't even arrested. Please!"

"Shut it!" was the disembodied answer.

"Can you at least send word to the deputy so we can get this cleared up sooner rather than later?"

"Shut it!"

"If Seamus Maloney murders more innocents, it will be on your conscience."

No response.

"Sheriff?"

Still nothing.

Jacob sighed deeply and backed away from the cell door. He sat dejected back on the cot. What else could he do? He racked his brain, trying to think of some option. The only thing that came to mind was to lure the sheriff back here and somehow trick and overpower him. But Jacob always—always—wanted to stay on the right side of the law and couldn't imagine himself ruining that streak just for this.

No, he would just have to be patient and—

Jacob heard something. Footsteps. He hurried to the cell door again and tried to peer down the hallway. Was the sheriff coming back already? Maybe he had found a note. Maybe he had—

Jacob heard the door to the office open, the sheriff exit and the door close again.

Through the closed door, he could also hear the sheriff's footsteps continue on down the wooden boardwalk.

"Damn it," Jacob whispered to himself. Now he was alone, locked up and at the mercy of whenever the sheriff or the deputy felt like showing up again. The only smidgen of hope he had was that Sheriff Whitaker had promised him meals. It was still morning, so maybe he'd come back with breakfast soon and Jacob could try reasoning with him again.

Several hours later, Jacob was still hoping the same thing. His stomach was beginning to growl and he wondered whether or not the sheriff had deliberately lied to him when he claimed to be providing meals to what he thought was a prisoner. Where had he gone? And where was the deputy?

Jacob had been pacing his cell while he waited. His adrenaline was up.

He hated being stuck. It was one of his worst fears and a big part of the reason he had left Virginia, after all. It wasn't claustrophobia; it was more that he liked to have options. And this being his first time ever locked in a cell only confirmed that preference.

It wasn't even just that he was physically stuck. Jacob hadn't made any progress on his manhunt at all the day before and now this new day was flying away too. If neither of the lawmen of this town could help him in his pursuit, who could Jacob turn to next? He began making mental lists of all the shops he remembered passing. He would interview every single citizen of this town if need be. Someone must have seen something.

The more time that passed, the more Jacob just wanted to yell and scream, to draw attention from someone walking by. Anyone.

He was trying to talk himself out of that impulse when the door to the jail finally opened again and Jacob heard two sets of footsteps enter.

"Hello? Sheriff, is that you? Can we talk?" Jacob yelled desperately.

"How many times do I have to tell you to shut it?" a familiar voice responded.

The footsteps continued toward Jacob, echoing through the hallway. He held his breath waiting to see the sheriff standing in front of him, hopefully with a key. Hopefully with Deputy Larson there to vouch for him.

Jacob couldn't help the grin spreading across his face when both men appeared in his view at the end of the hallway.

"Deputy!" he called. "Thank goodness. I'm so glad you're here. You've told the sheriff about your kind hospitality last night, I trust?"

"I sure have. Sorry about this, Mr. Payne. I didn't think." He mirrored Jacob's grin, shrugged and scratched his head. "Oh well. No harm done."

"I . . . but . . ." Jacob began to protest, but thought better of it. He was still stuck. Either man could still change their mind and then who knew when he would get out of here.

But as soon as the sheriff had unlocked and opened the jail cell, as soon as the deputy had handed him back his holster and weapon, and as soon as Jacob had safely and definitively stepped out into the hallway, he had to say something.

"Actually, Deputy, sorry, but there could be harm done." He tried to keep the bite out of his tone, but it was difficult. "As you may recall, I am still trying to hunt down the multiple murderer Seamus Maloney. My, uh, detention sacrificed important hours that I could have spent—"

"Yes, yes," Sheriff Whitaker said with a

dismissive wave as he led the way back down the hallway. "We get the idea. You should be grateful you got out at all, young man."

"Thank you," Jacob said through clenched teeth. "If I could bother you for another favor . . . do either of you have any more leads on Seamus Maloney's whereabouts? Other than your wife, deputy, who else has given you reason to believe they have seen this man in Haven?"

Jacob stood alert in front of the desk. Sheriff Whitaker had sat down, leaned back and rested his feet on the desk. Deputy Larson leaned casually against the wall behind him. As Jacob waited, his stomach growling broke through the silence. He would have to get some kind of sustenance in him if he was going to have energy for this manhunt.

"I think maybe Rufus?" the sheriff said in between picking at his teeth with a piece of paper he had picked up from his desk and folded into quarters. The man must have gone out for a meal while he had left Jacob here locked up. "What do you think, Grover?"

Deputy Larson nodded. "Yeah, I think Rufus is probably the best place to start."

"Who is Rufus?" Jacob asked.

"Runs the post office and general store here. A few buildings west of us," Deputy Larson said, gesturing with a point. "Marlowe's Goods is about the only place around here to get any kind of anything, so if Maloney has needed anything from bullets to flour, he's had to see Rufus."

"Great," said Jacob, immensely relieved. "That's perfect. I'll go see Rufus."

With that, he turned and abruptly exited the jail, before either man could detain him any further.

CHAPTER SIX

Once outside the jail, Jacob turned his steps toward where Deputy Larson had indicated, toward the general store, and hopefully toward some answers. He was still starving—it was just about lunchtime and he hadn't eaten anything all day. But he needed to get answers first. Once Jacob knew better where he was going and what he needed to do he could plan a meal. This wasn't the first time he had done the hard work while hungry. He had been a soldier, after all. He could handle this.

Larson had given him accurate directions, at least. Jacob found Marlowe's Goods four doors down from the jail. At this time of day, late morning, there were several women already there shopping. Jacob strolled casually around the aisles, trying not to interrupt, but still catch the eye of the short, scrawny man helping a customer at the counter. There was another shop assistant, a young man no older than seventeen, and several women waiting to be helped, but Jacob needed to speak to Mr. Marlowe himself as soon as possible.

Jacob would have to be patient. Again.

He wandered to the front window and watched the action in the street. There were just as many people walking and going about their day as he would expect in a town this size. Either Maloney wasn't here, or the word of his presence hadn't spread very far, or . . . Jacob sighed.

Maybe the people of Haven just weren't taking this outlaw very seriously. He had murdered seven people, and yet no one seemed to be showing any fear whatsoever. There was no indication a single person had altered their activities, other than Mrs. Larson bringing the school children inside. Jacob was furious at the cavalier way the law of this town was handling the situation and he was more determined than ever to bring this despicable man to justice.

He walked back to the counter, where the scrawny man was weighing out dried beans for his customer, and leaned on his elbow next to her.

"Excuse me, ma'am," he said when she eyed him doubtfully. "I'm here on business for the U.S. Marshal's office in Tucson. I hate to interrupt, but this is a matter of utmost importance."

The look of shock on the man's face was enough to sink Jacob's spirits. Was he going to have trouble getting this man to talk?

"Are you Mr. Marlowe?" he asked, extending his hand.

The man took his time sealing up the package of beans, giving his customer the total and completing the transaction before answering him.

"Excuse me, Mrs. Brown," he said to the next woman waiting. "I'll be just a moment."

Mrs. Brown glared at Jacob, clearly irritated her space in line had been usurped. He doffed his hat to her, but she looked away.

"Yes, I'm Rufus Marlowe," he said to Jacob. "What seems to be the trouble?"

"As I said, I'm here from Tucson. Jacob Payne. I understand that you may have interacted with a man the marshal's office is after."

Rufus paled visibly. "A wanted man? Have I? Oh, heavens. Oh, dear."

Jacob was concerned by the man's evident panic, but again he had to wonder how the law of this town was even functioning if a man of this stature didn't know there was an outlaw about.

"Possibly, Mr. Marlowe. I'm sorry to alarm you. It's possible I'm wrong." He pulled out the wanted poster Santos had given him with Maloney's likeness on it, unfolded it, and smoothed it out on the countertop. Then he shifted his position, trying to casually block the view of the poster from the other customers in the shop. He didn't want to be the cause of a panic.

"Is . . ." Marlowe cleared his throat. "Is that him then?"

Jacob nodded. "Does he look familiar?"

Marlowe had not taken his eyes off of the likeness, the gray-blond hair and sweeping mustache and goatee, the glaring eyes. He nodded.

"Has he come in here?" Jacob prompted.

Marlowe nodded again. He swallowed.

"You're not in any danger, Mr. Marlowe," Jacob said. "But if there's any info you can give me that might indicate where he has gone, or where he might be now, I'd surely appreciate it. The sooner I can get my hands on him, the sooner you and the people of Haven will be safe."

"He, um . . . he . . ."

Marlowe still had not taken his eyes off the wanted poster. Jacob needed him to focus; he gently lifted the storekeeper's hand off of the edge of the paper, folded it up and slipped it back into his pocket.

"Mr. Marlowe?"

Finally the smaller man looked up at Jacob.

"Do you want to get some air?"

He nodded. "Jack, I'll just be a moment. I need to help this gentleman with something."

The kid helping a diminutive older woman nodded to indicate he had heard. Marlowe gestured Jacob to follow him into the small storeroom in the back. As they walked between stacks of fabric bolts and barrels of sugar, Jacob wondered where Maloney was at that moment.

There was another door on the far side of the storeroom, and Marlowe made a beeline toward it. He opened the door into the sunshine and seemed to gulp in the fresh air. Stumbling forward, Marlowe left the door open and didn't give Jacob a second look. There was an old tree stump ten feet away and Marlowe collapsed onto it.

"Mr. Marlowe," Jacob said hesitatingly. "Are you okay? Can I do anything?"

The storekeep shook his head, and continued to take deep breaths. As Jacob watched, he seemed to be calming. Maybe all he needed was a minute to compose himself.

"I'm all right," Marlowe said. "I'm all right, I just . . . when I think about that man, I just . . ." His eyes widened again and his breathing became more erratic.

"Take your time," Jacob said, though he didn't really want to give the man any time. How much time had already been wasted? "Tell me what you know when you're ready."

Marlowe nodded. "I can. That is, I will. I just need . . ." He held up a single finger, as though to indicate one moment, and continued to take his deep breaths.

As he waited, Jacob looked around. Behind the store was a wide dirt alley. No, not even an alley. It was wide enough to be a street on its own; in any city back east this would be a waste of space between rows of buildings. About ten feet past the tree trunk where Marlowe was sitting was an outbuilding, and a house another several yards beyond that.

The organization and planning of Haven was haphazard at best. Which, to be honest, likely made hiding in plain sight even easier for Maloney. He could easily circumvent common meeting places and take alternate routes wherever he wanted to go.

"What's that fellow's name again?" Marlowe asked.

Jacob brought his attention back to the man in front of him. "Maloney. Seamus Maloney."

Marlowe shook his head. "No, I don't think that's the name he gave me. It was more like . . . Moore, actually. Mr. Moore. I'm not sure I got a first name."

"All right. When did you see him?"

"Th-this morning," he stammered. "He was in about an hour ago."

This additional piece of information made Jacob fume. If only the sheriff hadn't detained him in the jail, he could have already laid hands on the outlaw. He sighed. Well, there was nothing to do about it now.

"And he bought something from you?"

"Three boxes of bullets, a rope and two apples."

"Well. That's not great," Jacob said wryly. "Did he take the items with him? I don't suppose he gave you an address to deliver them to, did he?"

Marlowe shook his head. "No, he took it all

with him. I'm sorry. If I had known, I could have insisted."

That was precisely what Jacob had been thinking. If Marlowe had known. If anyone else in the town had known. Thank goodness Larson had thought to tell his wife, at least, so Santos heard about Maloney being in Haven. Without that lead, the outlaw could be halfway to California by now.

Jacob rubbed his temple. This was getting frustrating, but he had to stay focused.

"I understand. Not to worry, Mr. Marlowe. If there's anything else you can tell me—"

"When he left he went that way," the man said, pointing eagerly in the direction Jacob had just come from.

"Toward that end of town? Is there anything down that way that he might have mentioned, or . . . anything, Mr. Marlowe. I need to impress upon you the seriousness of this. There is no one else in this town I know to ask."

Marlowe looked surprised. "Well, the church is down that way. And the jail and the school. Some houses—"

"The church?" Jacob said. "It's not a Catholic church, is it?"

"No. Not Catholic."

"Does the reverend live near there?"

"Oh, yes. There's a parsonage just behind the church building. Reverend Chadwick was one of the first men to help settle this town."

Jacob wondered to himself what kind of man Maloney was. Sure, he murdered seven, maybe eight, people out of greed and desperation. But did he think of himself as a good person at his core? He may very well be the kind of outlaw who would confess his sins to save his soul and clear the slate—even if only to give himself free rein to commit some other heinous crime.

"Mr. Marlowe, could I ask you to do something for me?"

"Of course, Mr. Payne."

"If this man comes in again could you . . . I don't know where I'll be staying, but I'll drop in here as often as I can to see if there's any news. If you don't see me for a day or so, send a telegram to Tucson."

"Not tell the sheriff?"

"Well . . ." Jacob didn't want to undermine Whitaker's authority. "Sure. Tell the sheriff. But also tell the U.S. Marshal."

"I'll do that, sir. Thanks much. I . . ." He gulped. "I don't know how I'll keep my composure if he comes back, though."

"Maybe your assistant could help him?" Jacob suggested. "You can just observe."

"I'll try that. Of course," he said, brightening, "maybe you'll catch him before he comes back in here."

"Let's hope. I'll leave you to the rest of your day and your customers, Mr. Marlowe."

Jacob didn't look back as he strode away in the direction Marlowe had indicated.

CHAPTER SEVEN

Jacob all but ran down the street to the small Haven church. As he neared, he slowed, realizing that if Maloney was inside, he could be watching for him or ready to ambush anyone that sought after him. Jacob would need to seem as harmless as possible.

He remembered Marlowe's description of Reverend Chadwick's home, and looked for the parsonage that shared the same property as the church building. It was a small structure, behind the place of worship, but inviting. Jacob walked a wide arc, avoiding the church itself and followed the path to the front door of Reverend Chadwick's home.

When he knocked on the door, he heard giggling and shouting from within. A faint set of footsteps ran toward the door and it was flung open. A tiny, four-year-old girl with her blonde hair in pigtails stood grinning up at him. Jacob couldn't help but match her grin with his own.

"Hello!" she said loudly. "I'm Mary!"

Jacob laughed. "Hello, Mary. Is your father home?"

She shook her head, still grinning.

"Is your mother home?"

"Mary!" a voice called from down the hallway. In moments, a young woman with the same blonde curls as Mary came rushing towards the door. "I'm so sorry, sir, I had my hands full and . . ." She gestured wildly.

"It's really no trouble ma'am." Jacob removed his hat. "Are you Mrs. Chadwick by chance?"

"I am, yes. But I'm sorry I can't place you. You must be new to Haven."

"I am. That is . . . I'm passing through."

Mrs. Chadwick laughed. "Are you? That's new. No one just passes through Haven."

"Yes, well, I have . . ." Jacob glanced at Mary who was listening to every word. "I have some special circumstances. I was actually looking for your husband, ma'am. The Reverend Chadwick? He isn't here, is he?"

Mrs. Chadwick nodded. "He's in the church

at the moment. We've had another new face this week, and he seems to be needing a lot of guidance. Mr. Chadwick has been so gratified to see this man's devotion to the Scripture. I have no doubt they are in there together."

"Do you think it would be all right if I went in too? Would I be disturbing anything?"

"Oh, I'm not sure. Likely not. You seem like the kind of man who would be respectful if another was praying, wouldn't you?" She smiled at him. "I'm sure it will be just fine. You go on ahead."

"Thank you very much, Mrs. Chadwick," he said. "I'll leave you and Mary to whatever you were playing."

"Stagecoach," Mary said. "I'm gonna be a stagecoach driver when I grow up."

Jacob felt a small twinge of melancholy, thinking about this sweet child being on the stagecoach that Maloney had held up and massacred. He hoped none of his concern showed on his face. It wouldn't do for Mrs. Chadwick to begin asking questions.

"That sounds wonderful. What a fun game," he said with a smile. "I'm sure you'll be a great one."

Jacob made his good-byes and crossed the yard to the front double door of the church. It hadn't closed entirely the last time someone had passed through, and Jacob could hear the conversation going on inside.

"The Lord can forgive, Mr. Moore," the first voice said. It was melodic and soothing. Jacob could easily imagine this man preaching and expounding on the truth of the Bible every Sunday. "You just need to repent."

"I know, Father. I mean, Reverend," the second voice said. It was an older voice, tired and with the Irish brogue Jacob had expected to hear from Seamus Maloney. "But is repenting enough? 'Tis a fearsome thing I've done."

Jacob pressed his ear to the crack in the door, straining to hear every word.

"The Lord loves all his children. No matter what you've done."

"I dunno . . ."

"That is why he sent his son Jesus to die on the cross, after all, isn't it?"

"Well . . ."

"To wash away your sins."

"But, Father, what if I'm not sorry?"

Silence. Jacob felt his anger rise at such nonchalance.

The reverend cleared his throat. "What do you mean?"

"Well, see, I did this thing, that's true. But I

did it deliberately. I knew what I was doing and why."

"But now, though? Surely *now* you regret the sin—"

"That's what I'm saying, Father. I would do it again in a heartbeat. How can I claim to repent of something I would willingly do again?"

Jacob heard the reverend heave a deep sigh. He felt for the man. This was the leader of a congregation, trying to be helpful, trying to guide this man toward what he believed to be his salvation and everlasting life, and yet the man was resisting at every turn.

"What is it that you've done, Mr. Moore?" Reverend Chadwick asked quietly.

Silence again. Would the outlaw really admit to what he had done? Jacob pressed closer to the door, looking through the crack trying to see what the two men were doing.

Just when he thought he had the perfect angle, behind him the front door of the parsonage opened and a child's giggle startled him. In his turning to see, Jacob jostled the door to the church, pushing one side of the double door open and revealing his presence to the men inside.

If there had been any doubt in Jacob's mind,

it was gone the moment he stumbled through the doors of the church. Sitting side by side in the rear pews were two men, one about Jacob's age with dark brown hair and a neat mustache, and the other older, grizzled with the same blond-gray hair and blond-grey goatee as was depicted in the wanted poster Jacob was carrying at that very moment.

Both men looked up in surprise, and while Reverend Chadwick quickly calmed and smiled welcomingly at Jacob, Maloney stood in a panic.

"Freeze, Seamus Maloney," Jacob said, drawing his weapon. "In the name of the law. I'm taking you in."

"Like hell you are," Maloney said.

Reverend Chadwick gasped at such vulgarity.

The outlaw leaped over the back of the pew with the agility of a much younger man, and before Jacob realized what was happening, Maloney had pushed past him and was running down the street away from the church and away from him.

He was stuck. He couldn't shoot the man in the back. What kind of bounty hunter would he be if he did that? What kind of man would he be?

"Momma, what's happening?" a young voice

asked.

Jacob realized with a panic that the child was near to getting between him and the outlaw. He hadn't yet seen Maloney draw his weapon, but that didn't mean he hadn't or wouldn't. Jacob would never forgive himself if little Mary was injured in this skirmish.

"Get her back inside," he directed Mrs. Chadwick, who looked shocked at him. Jacob was worried she would be too surprised to take the action she needed to.

He picked Mary up with one arm and carried her bodily to Mrs. Chadwick's waiting embrace.

Next he turned his attention back to the outlaw running away from him.

"Stop that man!" he yelled as loudly as he could.

There weren't many people on the street at that time, and those that were likely saw that Jacob had drawn his revolver and wanted no part of this. He couldn't blame them. No average person could hope to confront an outlaw like this man and survive.

"Maloney!" he yelled. "You're only making this worse for yourself." He ran through the yard of the church, out to the middle of the street. "Stop!"

"You'll never catch me!"

Jacob ran, sprinted after the outlaw. He would never shoot a man in the back. There wasn't any situation when that would be okay with him. If Jacob couldn't get one of the other citizens to help stop Maloney, Jacob would have to go after him himself.

"Only a coward would run, Maloney! Turn around and face justice!"

"I am no coward."

The man turned. Aimed. Jacob heard the oath from the outlaw at the same time that the sound of gunfire broke through the air.

The pain that tore through Jacob's torso was red hot, like a poker stabbing through his gut. Surprised, he put a hand to his side and felt the warm sticky coating of blood spreading across his stomach and dripping down his side.

Jacob fell to his knees in the middle of the dirt street. Through the haze of his pain, he was dimly aware of Maloney escaping, of him running farther down the street, mounting a horse and disappearing. Which direction? Who would go after him?

Jacob struggled, stumbled, trying to get to his feet.

He collapsed again, face first, blood making mud of the dirt underneath him.

CHAPTER EIGHT

It must have been the pain that woke him up. The room was silent and dark with nothing to disturb him, but still Jacob felt himself regaining consciousness through the thick fog of burning pain.

He had been out west for more than six months, and in that time had almost never been shot. Not like this. Even during the war, his worst injuries were to his limbs, where the solid muscle could better bear the damage of a gunshot.

But this. This blow to his abdomen . . .

The door opened and the bright light of afternoon sun assaulted his eyes.

"Oh, I'm so sorry," a woman's voice said. "I didn't mean to disturb you."

As Jacob's eyes better adjusted to the dim light, he realized it was Mrs. Chadwick who had come into his sick room, carrying a basin of water and a towel.

"You're awake," she said. "How do you feel?"

She set the basin down on the table by his bed and wet the towel, wringing it out carefully before resting it on his forehead. The cool water was soothing, and distracted him a little from the pain.

"Sore," he croaked out. "How long have I been sleeping?"

"Not long. A few hours. Doc Harmon was here to get out the bullets and stitch you up again. Thank heavens you stayed unconscious for all of that. I couldn't even be in the room, with all the blood. My husband had to help the doctor."

She wetted the towel again, before replacing it on his forehead. He closed his eyes under the soft comfort of her touch.

"A few hours? What time is it?" Jacob tried to sit up. "What happened to the man that shot me?"

"Now, you lay back down, please, Mr. Payne," she said soothingly but commanding. She gently pushed his shoulder back toward the bed. "Sheriff Whitaker is just outside here and I can have him come in to talk to you. But you mustn't upset yourself."

Jacob lay back down. "The sheriff?"

"Promise me, Mr. Payne," she said. "We all want you to recover, which means you need to rest."

"I'll do my best. Sending the sheriff in to me will help."

She nodded, smiled, and left the room with the door open. Jacob heard murmurs of conversation outside the door and soon the light from the other room was blocked by the silhouette of Sheriff Whitaker.

"Well, son, Mrs. Chadwick tells me you wanted to see me."

"Can we— Is there a lamp in here, Sheriff? Can we get some light?"

"You don't need to sleep more? All right then, I think . . . Yes. Right here."

In a short moment, the kerosene lamp on the dresser across the room from Jacob illuminated a warm glow. Jacob looked down at his bandages. He was wound tightly all about his torso with wide, clean white fabric. His fingers probed; there were thick layers of padding over the gunshot wound. No blood yet had seeped through. Jacob experimented with taking deep breaths and didn't feel more than the pull of muscles. His lungs must not have been in the line of fire.

Jacob rested one hand on his stomach, right over the wound, imagining what his body must look like under all that protection.

"Sheriff, I assume the Chadwicks filled you in on what happened here earlier today. As I told you before, the marshal's office has sent me after this man, who has now shot me and escaped. Again." Jacob tried to keep the frustration out of his voice. "I need to know what you have done about it, or plan to do about it, so I can fulfill the marshal's request."

"Look here, Mr. Payne. Haven is my town and I'll be in charge of keeping the law here."

"That's fine," Jacob said with a sigh. "I don't aim to keep you from that, sir. And if you could see your way to not keep me from my job I'd appreciate it."

"I don't like your tone."

Jacob made himself wait a beat, take a breath, before continuing. "I apologize. It must be the pain is getting to me. I was just wondering if you could give me any more info about this outlaw."

The sheriff shook his head. "Way I understand it, he lit on outta here after trying to shoot up the church. We're lucky you're the only one who got a bullet."

Jacob nodded, grateful he had gotten little Mary out of the way when he did.

"Did you see anything?" he asked. "Anything at all? The direction, the . . . I don't know."

He felt helpless. Stuck. Again. In the pivotal moment when his prey was almost in his grasp he had not only lost him, but he had also lost consciousness and with it any chance of further information. Jacob was furious with himself, and frustrated. He couldn't be angry at the people of Haven. They were only trying to keep themselves safe, after all. He could, however, be angry with the sheriff.

"Did you see what he was wearing? What his horse looked like? Anything?"

The sheriff shook his head. "I'm sorry, Mr. Payne. We may just have to make due with knowing the man left Haven without causing any further damage."

"That may be enough for you," Jacob said, angrily. "But it is not enough for me."

He sat up, pushed back the blanket and put his feet on the floor. It was time for Jacob to get dressed again.

"We can agree that he left town, though?"

"Sure did," Sheriff Whitaker said eagerly. "West."

"West," Jacob repeated.

Assuming that was accurate, which at this point was anyone's guess, west was still a vast open expanse of desert. He stood, pulling on his pants, and reached next for his holster and belt. He almost lost his balance, and felt a stab of pain as his torn and wounded muscles worked to help him keep his balance. But he wouldn't stop. He couldn't rest. Jacob sat back onto the bed and reached for his boots.

"Could you pass those to me, please, Sheriff?"

Jacob finished gathering his belongings and getting dressed again almost in silence. He didn't have anything else to say to the sheriff who had seemed to be thwarting him at every turn. The reverend was kind enough to gift Jacob with a shirt, as his own had been bloodied and torn. Mrs. Chadwick insisted he take with him a small cold lunch—Jacob recalled he still hadn't eaten yet that day so he didn't protest her generosity too strongly. He said good-bye to little Mary, and made her promise to be good.

Finally, when he had gathered all of his things, he said his farewell to the sheriff, all but begging him to notify Tucson and Owen Santos if word of Maloney came through Haven again. Jacob hated that he sounded like he was begging but he didn't see any other way to make clear to the man the seriousness of the situation.

Injured, frustrated, hungry, tired and weak, Jacob still had to continue on his mission. He made his way to the livery to collect Blaze and begin his hunt again.

"You're heading out of Haven, sir?" Andy asked, as he got the horse saddled and ready for Jacob. "S'pose there's nothing to keep you here."

"That's right," Jacob agreed. "I'm on the trail of an outlaw, and it seems he has left town so I must too. I don't suppose you saw or helped a man with a big bushy blond mustache in the last couple days, did you?"

"Well, now, it just so happens that I did."

Jacob was shocked. Although now that he was here it made sense that the livery would have seen a new man coming to town, in his pessimism and frustration Jacob had given up hope anyone here would be willing to help him.

"You did? Did he— Was it this man?" Jacob hastily pulled out the wanted poster and showed Andy the likeness.

"Yes sir. That's him. Mr. Moore he said his name was though."

"I don't want to alarm you, but that's the man I'm after."

"Golly," Andy said, rubbing his chin thoughtfully. "He seemed so nice too. What'd you say he did?"

"I'm not sure that's important, seeing as he is no longer here. I wouldn't want to scare people unnecessarily."

"I understand."

"Is there anything else you can tell me?" Jacob asked. "The direction he went? If he said anything about his plans? Any identifying characteristic that can help me track him down."

"I'm not sure . . ." He stared off into space and scrunched up his face as though trying to remember.

"Anything, Andy. Any detail you can give me. We never know when something is going to be useful."

"Well, now . . . since you mention it, yes, actually, mister. Mr. Moore—uh, Maloney—had me put this blanket under the horse's saddle. I ain't never seen anything like it."

"A blanket?"

"Yessir. A woven blanket that he told me he got from a savage."

"A native?" Jacob clarified.

"Uh-huh. I dunno if that was the truth or

not. But I also heard him talking about Santa Fe and Austin, so maybe he got it somewhere else and just hadn't put it on the horse yet."

"Can you remember what it looked like?"

Andy scrunched up his face again with the effort of remembering. "Purpley. With black and white and gray. Kinda blocky, I guess. I dunno. I'm not much one for fashion."

"No, that's great. That's perfect. And you say he went west?"

"Yes, sir. I saw him hop up on that gelding and git just a few hours ago."

Jacob took a deep breath. This was better than he had hoped. And it was better than nothing.

"You've been very helpful, Andy. I can't thank you enough."

"My pleasure, Mr. Payne."

As Jacob rode out of Haven, west toward the lowering sun, he cursed his luck. The entire interlude in town had been nearly futile. True, he had confirmed that Maloney had been there, at least. And even laid eyes on him. But he had been sent in circles, no one in town, least of all the sheriff, willing to do anything about the fact that they had a notorious murderer in their midst.

And if that hadn't been enough, Jacob had

been shot. This injury would heal, and he thanked God it wasn't worse than it was. But it would certainly hold him back. If the next leg of his search for Maloney required anything physical from him, he could be in trouble.

Jacob thought over his options. He mulled over what he knew about Maloney, and what he knew about this part of the territory. At the moment the best piece of information he had to go on was that the man had traveled west, so that's what he was doing too. West on the only road leading out of Haven. West toward . . . well, he wasn't sure what.

CHAPTER NINE

Jacob and Blaze continued their trek west. Each jostle brought him pain, but he couldn't stop yet. Maloney was still on the loose and Jacob didn't trust for a moment that he was done with his path of destruction. The afternoon wore on, and Jacob had more than one occasion to be irritated that the sheriff of Haven had so delayed him that morning. The bounty hunter tried to gauge how many hours of sunlight he had left and what his plan would be once he could no longer see to travel. He would go as far as he could, hindered only by his own hunger and tolerance for pain.

When he was only an hour outside of Haven, Jacob noticed a ranch in the distance, maybe half a mile off the main road. It was the only civilization for miles. From this distance it looked deserted other than the horses milling around the corral. But there was something—something small, something he almost missed—that caught his eye.

Jacob peered toward the ranch, uncertain if he had seen what he thought he saw. Was it possible what he was looking for, what he had been prepared to travel all over the desert for, would be right in front of him?

He directed Blaze down the long path toward the ranch. As each step brought him closer, he tried to catch a glimpse of what had drawn his attention before. That color. That hint.

When he was just a hundred yards from the house, he stopped. Most of the landscape was small dry shrubs and saguaro cactus, but whoever lived here had put additional work into building up their homestead. A small group of trees along the track from the main road offered Jacob a little concealment. He dismounted and lead Blaze to the shade on the far side.

From that distance, he looked again. His suspicions were confirmed. One of the horses in the corral had snagged his attention. There, under the saddle just as Andy had described, was a purple woven blanket. Jacob's thoughts echoed what the man had said: he had never seen anything like it.

There was no question. That horse was the same one Maloney had ridden off on. This ranch could be where the outlaw was hiding out. For a brief moment, Jacob was grateful for his luck. But then he recalled what the outlaw must be after to stop at the one residence outside of the town. Jacob needed to get in there and capture the man as soon as possible.

Jacob watched the ranch for at least twenty minutes, waiting for something to happen. All he had to go on was seeing that purple woven blanket under the saddle of one of the horses. Why the horse had been left to roam around the corral still with a saddle on, Jacob could only guess. Likely Maloney intended to take what he needed and escape again.

In which case, Jacob only had to watch long enough to see him leave.

The bullet wound in his side throbbed with pain. Jacob vowed to himself that the first thing he would do once Maloney was in custody, was allow himself a rest. He wouldn't be fool enough to think he was invincible, and he'd be no use to Santos if the hole in his side didn't heal.

Jacob sighed deeply, frustrated. Resting was the last thing he wanted to do.

At least he wouldn't have to do it yet.

As the sun dropped lower in the sky, Jacob expected to see one or two of the windows light up from within. If everything was safe and secure at the ranch, if he was mistaken about whose horse that was, Jacob could expect to see at least one of the residents of the ranch going about an evening chore. Coming out to draw water from the well, or bringing in fuel for the stove. Maybe one of the men returning home from a day working the farther reaches of the property.

But as Jacob watched, his suspicions grew. There was no movement. None at all, other than the horses still left alone in the corral outside the barn.

From this distance, Jacob couldn't expect to hear anything, but he should be able to see something. Light. Movement. Anything. He wished he knew who lived in this ranch and what he should be looking for.

He wished, once again, that he had something more to go off of. That the people of Haven had been more helpful. Surely with a ranch this close to town, the family living here must be known to the sheriff or the general store or the reverend. Surely someone in Haven could have told him about this residence closest to town.

Instead, Jacob was going in blind.

But, at least he wasn't stuck again.

The situation in Haven, being locked into the jail with no recourse, had frustrated him more than he liked to admit. Jacob had always been independent, never liking to ask for help. Now, thank goodness, he didn't have to worry about that. If he was right in his suspicions, if Maloney was inside that ranch house, then Jacob could do what he does best and apprehend the outlaw.

Once he knew better what he was dealing with, he could formulate his plan.

The door to the ranch house opened and Jacob was immediately alert. There was still no light within the building, so all he could see was the barest suggestion of a silhouette. It appeared to be a man, hatless. Jacob held his breath and tried to shrink farther into the shadows of the trees. If he were spotted at this juncture, all would be lost.

After a beat, Jacob realized the man was not alone. Another figure was pulled out of the building with him. With the little Jacob could see, this second person also appeared to be male, but a bit shorter than the first man, and less broad across the shoulders. A boy, maybe.

The man handled the boy roughly, holding his upper arm in a grip and all but dragging him down the steps from the house and across the property.

So much Jacob didn't know, and so little he could see from this small interaction.

The man dragged the boy across the dirt to the barn, opened the door and pushed him through. The man himself followed for a brief couple minutes and Jacob was going crazy imagining all the things that could be happening behind that door.

Not long after, though, the man appeared again alone, closed the barn door, and jammed the handle of a shovel through the door handles, effectively locking it.

Whoever he had left inside the barn, he didn't want to get out.

The man turned back to walk towards the house. When he turned in Jacob's direction, the bounty hunter could clearly see the man's gray-blond hair and gray-blond mustache. It was Maloney.

There was no doubt whatsoever.

When Jacob saw that, he knew what he had to do, and quickly. He was losing daylight.

In only a few more steps, Maloney was back in the ranch house. If Jacob was going to make it to the barn without being seen he would have to run. He'd have to run all while avoiding the windows of the ranch house. It would be challenging but not impossible.

He secured Blaze, making sure the horse was as far out of sight as he could manage with his reins wrapped around a tree branch. He checked his weapons, making sure to be as armed as possible in case the worst happened. And he took a long drink of water. The cool liquid gave him a boost of energy that he would need if he was going to be able to make this sprint with the hole in his side.

Dropping his hat and everything extra he could, Jacob took one last searching look at the building within which Maloney had disappeared. He didn't detect any movement within, but without any lamp lit he couldn't be sure.

He took a deep breath.

Then he ran.

Jacob ran straight toward the house. He sprinted across the dirt road, bounced over the split rail fence and crossed diagonally through the corral. The shortest distance to the side of the building was directly between the horses. As Jacob ran, he could feel his blood pumping harder. He knew his wound would start to bleed through his bandage if he had to keep this up much more. But still he ran, focused on his objective, ready to draw his revolver the second he saw Maloney.

Four more steps. Three. Two. One long final step and he was to the house. Jacob ducked down below the windowsill and tried to catch his breath. It was difficult to listen to what was going on within the house while he was breathing so heavily, but the sound of heavy footsteps on the floorboards was unmistakable.

Without knowing the layout of the house, Jacob couldn't even begin to guess what he was doing in there, though he knew it was nothing good. Without knowing what Maloney could be up to or what resources he had at his disposal, Jacob was loath to confront him.

No, the best step would be to free the young man he now knew to be imprisoned within the barn, pump him for information, and make a new plan from there.

CHAPTER TEN

Jacob listened hard. That sound—Maloney walking around the house—seemed to be receding. The ranch house wasn't large, but if the outlaw wasn't near the windows closest to Jacob, he had a chance. He looked around the corner of the house to where the barn lay on the far side. He would have to make another run for it. He was just barely catching his breath, but he couldn't wait any longer.

He put his hand to his side and felt the beginnings of sticky blood starting to soak through to his shirt. That meant it had already gone through the bandage. He sighed. Maybe he could . . . he didn't know. He couldn't think of a solution for his own injury until he had been sure to save the kid, and whoever else the murderer might have trapped here. Jacob knew he wouldn't die from the wound. It was stitched up. He wouldn't lose enough blood for him to worry about it yet.

He had to move.

As soon as he ascertained that Maloney wasn't anywhere near his side of the building, Jacob took off in a sprint again, this time ducking low to try to stay out of view from the home's windows. He dug down to find reserves of energy he didn't think were there and ran, past the well, past the porch until he reached the barn.

The door to the barn was in the direct line of sight of the ranch house, so Jacob had to move quickly. In one fluid motion, he pulled the shovel out of the door handles, opened the barn doors just enough so that he could slip through, and stepped into the darkening structure. As soon as the barn door was closed behind him, Jacob could hear what else was in there with him.

It took his eyes a moment to adjust to the darkness, but soon Jacob could make out the shapes of not one, but four people. The sound he was hearing was the muffled protests as each of the shapeless forms yelling and crying while still gagged.

Jacob held his hands up so they could all see he wasn't holding a weapon. Though he couldn't make out any words, the sounds were clearly those of fear.

"I'm here to help," he said in a whisper. "I'm a bounty hunter from Tucson, here to capture the man that has tied you up."

The muffled cries he heard then changed their tone. No longer afraid, he sensed relief in the room as the captives heard his promise.

Jacob darted to the closest person, sitting awkwardly, leaning into a loose pile of hay just cast against the wall. It was a young girl; she couldn't be any older than six or seven. Close in age to Mary Chadwick, he thought with a pang. She had evidently been rolling around in the hay, trying to get herself free, because there were straws sticking through her brown hair in several directions.

Jacob pulled the gag down with one hand and held a finger to his lips with the other, reminding the girl to be quiet.

"Are you hurt?" he whispered.

She shook her head and started crying. Bawling.

"Shhh, shhh shhh," he said, moving to untie her hands. "I know. I'm sorry. I know this is scary, but you need to stay quiet so the man doesn't come back."

The girl nodded and closed her lips tight. Tears still poured down her face, cutting tracks in the layer of dirt there, but she managed to stay quiet.

"Good girl. My name is Jacob. What's yours?"

"Bonnie," she said in a loud whisper.

"Bonnie?" His voice caught in his throat. "Your name is Bonnie?"

She nodded.

"That's a lovely name." He was shaken. This poor helpless creature tied up and gagged was bad enough, but picturing his own Bonnie in such a situation nearly broke his heart. Jacob stood up again, now that she had been untied. "If you're not hurt, let me go help one of these others, all right?"

She nodded again and wiped her face, dragging the streak of dirt sideways.

Jacob turned his attention to the next closest—it seemed to be the same young man he had seen Maloney just drag into the barn. At this close distance, Jacob could see he was likely fifteen or sixteen years old. Practically a man. As soon as the gag was pulled down, he sputtered angrily.

"I'll kill him! I'll—"

"Shhh," Jacob warned, less kindly this time. This young man should know better. "You're not killing anyone. I need your help. What's your name?"

"George Thatcher," the kid said sullenly.

"George Thatcher," Jacob repeated, as he untied the binding from around his wrists. "I need you to tell me what happened here. What are we dealing with?"

"That man," he said, rubbing the raw skin of his wrist.

"Untie someone while you talk," Jacob said as he interrupted him. The final two people tied up in the barn were both young ladies, both younger than George. Jacob was surprised and pleased by the way the girls stayed calm all while he and George freed him, and the young man told his story.

"That man showed up here, I dunno, a few hours ago and just— He just—"

"I can imagine," Jacob said, trying to be soothing. "Where are your parents?"

"They're still inside," George said.

All four children were free now, but Jacob kept them close, sitting on hay bales inside the barn, away from the door and keeping their voices low for now. The oldest girl sat between the two others and tried to comfort them. George seemed too agitated to even sit, let alone notice his siblings.

"So this man comes, and he somehow manages to corral the whole family?" Jacob couldn't imagine the damage this outlaw must have doled out to have accomplished that. The risks he must have taken. The cold-hearted threatening.

"As far as I can tell," George said, "he got us all one at a time. He musta been watching and waiting and . . . I worry for my ma, you know? All the girls were in here, but when I was I the house, the man had separated our parents into different rooms, and Ma . . . she . . ."

He trailed off, then shook his head as though he couldn't speak any more.

"I understand. Let me just ask a few more questions. Other than you four, and your parents in the house, is there anyone else on the land? Any hired help that might walk into an ambush, or—"

"No, sir. It's just us. The Thatcher family all take care of ourselves," he said proudly.

"Well, that's good, then," Jacob said approvingly. "Fewer people to come to harm."

"Excuse me, sir?" the oldest of the girls said. "Is this a . . . a bad man?"

Jacob softened. "What's your name?"

"Eliza."

"Well, Eliza, I'm glad you asked that. He is a bad man, but that's why I'm here. So he can't do any more bad things. I just need you to trust me and everything will work out fine."

She nodded, and held tight to both of her sisters' hands.

"Now, George," Jacob said, turning his attention to the boy. "What can you tell me about the weapons your father has on hand?"

"Well, this man probably found 'em."

"All of them?"

George's face slowly lit up. "No, you're right. Not all."

"Are there any weapons stored or hidden outside the house that we can still get to?"

George nodded. "You bet! I can take you!"

"That's great, George." Jacob smiled at his enthusiasm. "Your help will be really instrumental in getting your parents freed. I have an idea, and I'd like if you helped me."

"Course I will."

Jacob turned to the three sisters, who were sitting and listening.

"Girls, I think you will probably be safest in here."

The middle girl shook her head, afraid. "No, please."

"I'm sorry," Jacob said. "But if you stay in here you can stay out of his sight, and maybe if George and I can distract or capture the other man, he'll forget all about you. Now that you're untied, you should be able to run and hide in the deep recesses of the barn if you need to as well."

Eliza nodded. "He's right, Sarah. We'll be okay."

"I don't wanna."

"Where do you want to go instead?" Eliza asked her sister.

She shrugged. "With Ma and Pop."

"They'll be here soon," Eliza said, putting an arm around her. "We need to stay hidden and safe for them, though, okay?"

Sarah didn't respond, but she had stopped protesting.

"You all have been very brave," Jacob said. "We'll get through this. I just need you to make sure to follow my instructions no matter what. Is that clear?"

All four of the children nodded solemnly.

CHAPTER ELEVEN

The sun had just set behind the horizon when Jacob finished explaining to George how they would set about freeing his parents. Working without light would make the entire enterprise more fraught with danger, but would also afford them cover. George knew the ranch far better than Maloney would, and so Jacob put his bet on the boy. He needed to get this man into custody as soon as possible. He had already killed, injured, or otherwise hurt far too many people and Jacob couldn't have anyone else becoming a victim.

Maloney would not be leaving the Thatcher ranch except under Jacob's control.

Eliza had calmed her younger sisters, and settled them into a far corner of the barn where they could wait and relax as best possible. He was sure they would worry, but he trusted they wouldn't give the game away by crying out or interfering with what he and George were setting out to do.

"As soon as we know it's safe, we'll come back for you," Jacob said in a whisper to the girls. "If Maloney comes for you before I do, scream. Scream as loudly as you can and run and fight. I know you can do it. All three of you together can keep each other safe. Promise me."

The three girls nodded eagerly. Jacob was satisfied they knew what to do. He could turn his focus to their parents.

The first thing he and George needed to do was to uncover the other weapons that the boy thought to be hidden on the ranch. The barn was one of the farthest outbuildings from the ranch house. Approximately fifty yards away was a shed that George claimed was full of the tools his mother and the girls used for the vegetable garden.

"Last I saw there was a rifle in there, up on one of the high shelves. And extra bullets. Pa has kept it there to shoot the jackrabbits that had been getting into the lettuce."

"How long ago was that?"

George shrugged. "Spring time. Six months, maybe?"

Jacob nodded, thinking. Hopefully the weapon was still there. He would have to trust to George's word on whether or not he was a good shot. But even if he couldn't hit the broad side of a barn, Maloney didn't know that. Jacob didn't want to be bringing the boy in to any situation unarmed.

He cracked open the barn door just an inch, just enough to see out. The angle wasn't exactly right to see the shed, but George could direct them.

"It's just around the corner there."

Now that the sun had fully set, there was a lamp lit within the house. It was in a front room. The curtains were drawn, so Jacob couldn't see in to what was happening, but it was clear that the activity was happening in there.

"That's my parents' bedroom," George said in a whisper. "What is he doing to them?"

"We'll find out," Jacob reassured him. "Just as soon as we have that weapon for you."

George nodded. "I'm ready."

"Okay. Follow my lead."

The room with the lit lamp was, fortunately, on the opposite corner of the house from where they needed to run. If they could be quiet enough and quick enough, Jacob believed they could get to the shed without being seen. He took one last look to the corner where the girls were sitting, satisfied that they had all but blended in with the dark corner, and turned his attention back to the barn door.

"Don't forget to close the door behind you," he whispered to George.

With that, Jacob slipped through the narrow opening and began running around the ranch house to where he knew the shed should be. As soon as he rounded the corner, he saw it. The building couldn't be more than six foot squared, but that was big enough. Jacob sprinted the final few yards to the structure, and behind it. He needed to be sure he could unlock and open the shed door before he dawdled on the side facing the house.

George was right behind him. "Made it."

Jacob nodded, staying as quiet as possible. He peeked around the corner. From this side of the house, he couldn't see the lit room at all. Which meant he really had no idea if Maloney was in any of the rooms on this side of the house.

There was so much at stake, so much Jacob was risking, but what choice did he have.

"You know how to open this door?" he whispered.

"Yup. I'll do it."

"As fast as you can."

George disappeared behind the building, leaving Jacob to wait breathlessly for confirmation he had gotten in. In moments, there was a light knock on the wall in front of him, where George was on the other side.

Jacob took the cue and darted around the building himself, through the door and closed it behind him. As soon as the door latched shut, the small building was pitch black dark. They could only feel their way around the room.

"I found it!" George whispered triumphantly.

"Good. And the ammunition?"

"That's here too. I wish we could light a lamp. There's probably lots of other good stuff in here we can use."

"True," Jacob whispered. "But I'm not willing to take that risk. Are you?"

"No, sir. What's next?"

"Now we have to figure out where Maloney is and how to get into the house."

"The backdoor is right there," George whispered excitedly.

"Does it have a lock?"

"Not yet. Pop keeps saying no one will bother us way out here."

"I see." Jacob wondered how this trauma would affect the family going forward, but maybe a lock on the door would make them feel more secure. "That's good news for us, then. If we can confirm that Maloney is still on the other side of the house, we can sneak in through the back and surprise him."

"How do we do that?"

"We listen."

Jacob felt his way to the door of the shed, fingers nudging along the edge of the door. He pushed it open just an inch, another tiny sliver he could use to see as much as possible. Jacob reminded himself that he had been in positions like this before. Maybe not precisely, maybe not with a sixteen year old kid as his help. Maybe not with the volatile unknown of a multiple murderer. But he had often found himself in situations where he knew little or nothing, and had to make precarious decisions.

This was nothing.

He could do this.

As he examined the house, he noted again that no interior light was visible on this side of the house.

"What rooms are those?" Jacob asked George in a whisper.

"The backdoor goes right into the kitchen. That window on the right is the pantry just off the kitchen. I sleep there on a cot, but otherwise Ma only goes in there for ingredients. The window on the left is the bedroom where the girls sleep."

"All right," Jacob said to himself. "The kitchen worries me. If he's feeling hungry or thirsty after whatever deeds he's doing in there, he could easily wander into the kitchen looking for something. Maybe without a lamp. Maybe he brings the lamp with him and we don't see it in time."

George was silent a moment before asking, "So what do we do?"

Jacob stood up straighter and squared his shoulders. "We go in anyway."

He could wait and watch all night, but he could never be absolutely certain of what he would be walking into. Better to just go, take action, and figure out what to do as he went.

Hunched over, nearly bent in half and exacerbating the bullet wound in his side, Jacob ran. The distance between the shed and the back of the house was only twenty yards or so, but that would be plenty for Maloney to see them if he happened to be glancing out the window at the right moment. If Jacob could stay low, below the windowsills, they had a better chance.

He hoped George thought to do the same thing.

Jacob ran so fast he almost slammed into the back siding of the house; he couldn't slow quickly enough. He cursed under his breath. Maloney was sure to have heard that thump of his shoulder against the wood. He drew his weapon, ready, aiming it at the back door for the moment the outlaw came out to check.

George was right behind him, fortunately stopping before he too slammed into the building. The young man saw what Jacob was doing and also held his weapon ready. The two of them were armed, on guard, and pointed at the back door of the house.

After a short moment of waiting, Jacob began to think he had caught a break. Maybe Maloney was too busy yelling or otherwise harassing George's parents to have paid attention to some sound from outside. Maybe he was lulled into thinking he was secure, since this ranch was so far out of town.

Maybe Jacob had a chance.

He glanced at George, nodded to indicate they were going forward, and crept the few feet between him and the back door of the house. He put his hand on the doorknob and turned it slowly. Slowly. It was in good order and made almost no sound. Jacob held his breath as he pulled the door open, bit by bit, and was again relieved to find that the hinges didn't squeak, the door didn't creak. There was no big noise to give them away.

Jacob was quick, into the house, into the dark kitchen, still ducking low to keep his silhouette as small as possible. Maloney could be watching from anywhere.

He took a few steps into the room and listened. He held his breath as George entered the house right behind him, but try as he might Jacob couldn't hear any indication of any activity happening elsewhere in the house.

It was bigger than he expected, but still not so big that they couldn't expect to hear a commotion just a room or two away.

He took a few more steps into the kitchen, slowly to keep his boots from making too much noise on the floorboards. His revolver was ready; he expected Maloney to appear around the corner any second.

But the silence unnerved Jacob. What was happening in here?

He shot George a puzzled look, then turned

back to walk farther into the house. In just a couple steps, he was in the doorway, looking down the hallway toward the bedrooms.

The lamp was still lit in the front room, in George's parents' room, in the room where he had believed the two adults were being held captive. But still he heard nothing. Not even a muffled protest of someone crying through a gag.

Nothing.

Jacob shook his head. He didn't like this. Not one bit.

CHAPTER TWELVE

Jacob peered down the dark hallway toward the lit room and listened. He could have listed at least a dozen different sounds that he would have expected, but not a single one of them met his ears. Not footsteps, not crying, not even the sound of a murderous outlaw's heavy breathing.

All he heard was George in the darkness next to him.

Jacob would have to check it out.

He stepped cautiously, quietly, resolutely down the empty hallway. Only ten feet, but ten feet of thick tension. As Jacob got near enough to the door of the bedroom to see in, he slowed even more.

Just inside the doorway was a bureau, a heavy wooden set of drawers that must have been very important to the family to have been brought all the way out from the east. As Jacob took several more steps forward, he spotted the corner of the bed. He paused. He braced himself for what he might be about to see.

And yet still he heard nothing coming from the room.

Jacob walked the final several steps until he was standing in the very doorway of the bedroom, his weapon drawn, ready and aimed at . . .

Nothing. There was no one in the bedroom.

He cursed under his breath.

At least, there wasn't anyone there anymore. There had been, however. Of that Jacob was sure. The chaos and mess left behind were a clear signal that Maloney had used this room for nefarious deeds.

"What?" George said from just behind Jacob. He walked around the bounty hunter into the center of the room and turned in a circle. "Where are they? Where are my parents?"

"Quiet, now," Jacob admonished as he looked around the room. "We don't know where Maloney is either. We've gotta keep a clear head about this."

George collapsed onto the bed. "What do we do now?"

"We look for clues. Tell me what you see. The bed has been used. What else? What is different?"

"I don't know. I almost never come in here."

"Look, George. You've got to help me. You're the only one that can do this."

He nodded, sighed, stood up and looked around again.

The bed was a mess. A quilt had been pulled off and was cast over the footboard of the bed and mostly on to the floor. A plain sheet still covered the mattress, but only over three of the corners. A struggle had occurred there, pulling the sheet away from one of the corners. Jacob took a few steps farther into the room and noticed another sheet on the floor next to the bed.

George saw it too. He bent down to pick it up and both men realized it was only part of a sheet. At least a third of the piece of fabric had been ripped off. Jacob cringed inwardly, sure that the torn-off fabric had been used to detain the Thatchers.

On the floor near the wall, next to the side of the bed, Jacob noticed a few tiny dark spots. He crept closer to look, and found drops of blood on the floorboards near the wall. Not many. Not enough to signal a bullet wound or elaborate fight. Maybe one of the parents had been bludgeoned or punched and this small bloodletting was the result.

Jacob moved away, before George could notice what he was looking at, but he wasn't quick enough. The boy saw it right away and gasped.

"What happened? What happened here? Whose blood is this?"

"Let's not panic," Jacob said, putting his hand on the other's shoulder. "That's not enough blood to worry."

"Not enough to worry? How can you say that? Of course I'm worried! What has that man done to my mother?"

"Hopefully nothing," Jacob said, though in his heart he knew they couldn't count on that. "That's why we need to keep looking for clues. We need to know what happened here. And where he has taken them. What else do you see?"

George's searching of the room became frantic now. Jacob stepped to the doorway and looked down the hallway, anxious that Maloney might be nearby and hear them.

"Here," George said.

When Jacob went to look, the teenager was standing in the opposite corner of the room, near the bureau.

"All of this." He gestured to the floor. "This was all on top of the drawers. It got knocked off."

Jacob looked to see a framed photo and a cracked porcelain dog figurine on the floor. Damage, yes, but again it didn't indicate what could have happened to the couple.

"Good. That's good, George. So we know there was a struggle here. Likely your father fought back. You should be proud of him."

"But then what happened?"

"We know they were in here long enough that he needed to light the lamp. We know one of your parents was injured, though not badly. And we know they're gone now."

Jacob sighed and walked back across the room, looking for a clue or sign he had missed.

"Were there any weapons in here?" he asked George.

"Oh! Yes! Let me— " George fell to his knees to look under the bed. "No. It's gone."

"I'm not surprised," Jacob said. "That would have been the first thing that Maloney got out of them." He turned and paced back across the room the other way.

"What else would he have done?"

Jacob kept his back to George, not wanting to entertain any speculation into what a man like Maloney might have done. Short of murdering them, it could have been anything.

"George, let me ask you something. I noticed there weren't any horses in the barn when we were in there. Where else does your family keep your animals?"

He shrugged. "Just the corral. Unless someone is riding one, but that's not happening right now."

"Good. That's what I thought. Let's check. Come here next to me."

Jacob crossed the room to the window, but stayed to the right side of it. With the room lit from within, he knew that he could be a sitting target to anyone outside looking in. He cupped his hands to the glass and looked out, toward the corral.

It was quite dark out now, but Jacob could just barely make out Blaze across the ranch and tied under the tree by the road. The only reason he could see the horse was because he knew exactly where to look.

Between him and Blaze was the corral, where Jacob counted five horses, including Maloney's.

"George, do you see that? The horses in the corral. Is that all of your family's animals?"

"Let's see . . ." George also cupped his hand to the glass to look out. "Yes, that looks like all of them."

"So, Maloney hasn't left yet. He must still be on the property."

"But where?"

Just as Jacob was about to withdraw from the window, a small glint of light caught his eye. Somewhere nearby another lamp had been lit. Taking care to stay as close to the edge of the glass as possible, Jacob swiveled his view to look out the other direction.

The small bit of light was coming from an open door. Jacob squinted, trying to adjust his eyes to the light.

"No," he whispered. "George, we have to go."

"What? What is it?"

"Did you remember to close the barn door when we left?"

"I . . . Yes. I'm sure of it. Or, I think I did. I must have." George pressed his face harder to the glass. "What is it?"

"Do you see that light?"

"Yes. I— Oh no! My sisters! We have to go save them."

"We will. We must."

Both men left the window and hurried out of the bedroom. George elbowed Jacob out of the way in his haste to get to the home's front door.

"George, wait!"

"But, my sisters!"

The anguished look on his face when he turned back to face the bounty hunter broke Jacob's heart. The poor boy just wanted to help his family. But it was Jacob's responsibility to make sure he didn't also get hurt in doing so.

"George, we don't know what we're walking into," he said sternly. "We have to assume Maloney is in there with them, with your parents and your sisters trapped, maybe hurt, we don't know. Remember, we didn't hear the girls scream. Who knows what could have happened? But, you have to remember. This is my job. This is what I am good at. I need you to trust me and to listen to me. I need you to follow every instruction I give you without hesitation and without arguing. Am I clear?"

"But what if—"

"Without arguing. You will be no good to your family if you are injured or killed. Trust me to keep that from happening."

"But—"

"George. Promise me."

He sighed deeply and dejectedly. "All right. Fine. Fine. I promise. But can we go now?"

"Yes. We'll go now. We'll run across the yard to the barn as quickly as we can, then wait outside the door for me. We need to assess what we're dealing with before we just walk in there guns blazing. We don't want anyone getting hurt."

"Yeah, okay. I understand. Let's just go."

Jacob nodded and let the boy lead the way down the hallway to the front door. He had a bad feeling about this. Knowing that the safety of the whole family was in his hands was bad enough, but with as anxious as George was, Jacob wasn't sure he could keep the boy reined in.

"Ready?" George said, looking over his shoulder to the other man.

Jacob nodded, gun in hand. They stepped out the front door into the dark night.

CHAPTER THIRTEEN

As Jacob exited the ranch house to make his way toward the barn, George pushed past him to begin running.

For the second time that day, Jacob heard the crack of gunfire.

He dropped, crouching on the porch of the ranch house and protecting himself as best he could behind one of the posts. George was already down the steps and several feet away from the house when he too dropped to the ground.

The cry of pain from the young man, however, told Jacob something else was wrong.

A second crack of gunfire tore through the air, but Jacob couldn't tell where it landed. A third gunshot fired, and the wooden beam above his head splintered.

"Don't come a step closer!" he heard shouted across the dark property.

"George!" Jacob yelled. "Are you hit?"

The young man groaned. "My arm! I can't believe it!"

"Stay right there."

Maloney had stopped yelling, and when Jacob looked up, he noticed the barn door had been closed tightly. Hopefully with the outlaw inside. Jacob needed to act fast. He didn't like thinking what the man might be doing with the rest of the family all captive in there, especially now that he knew that someone else was on the ranch and coming after him.

Trapped men did desperate things, and Jacob couldn't handle any other injury to this family on his conscious.

In a crouching run, Jacob hustled to where George lay in the dirt, clasping his right arm.

"How does it feel? Can you make a fist?"

George continued to groan and cry, holding his arm out from his body as though it were a thing separate from him. Jacob guessed this was the first time this boy had ever been shot.

"You'll be all right. Do you hear me? This

will be fine, but you can't come with me anymore."

"No, I have to." George tried to stand, but Jacob held him firmly down.

"Absolutely not. Your shooting arm is injured and you are going to lose a lot of blood if we don't get that bandaged up right now."

"But—"

"Look, George. You promised me that you would listen to what I say. That you would follow my instructions without questioning, remember? You promised. Now is the time to do that."

"Oh . . ." He groaned again.

"Let's get you inside before either one of us gets shot again."

There was another shot of gunfire, and both men ducked down to the ground.

"Are you hit?" Jacob asked.

George paused a moment before answering, but shook his head.

"I don't like this," Jacob said. "He's getting clumsy. He's bound to hurt someone else. Let's get you inside so this can all be over."

George nodded and wrapped his good arm around Jacob's shoulders, allowing the other man to help him to his feet. The two returned the ten feet into the dark ranch house and Jacob helped him to a chair in the kitchen.

"Do you know where your mother keeps the supplies?"

"In there." George indicated with his head. "That cupboard. There's a box— Yeah, that's the one," he said as Jacob pulled out the case.

He had bandaged up plenty of bullet wounds. He had even done it in faster, more desperate situations than this. Jacob made quick work of it, in spite of having to pause often to hush George. He was just a boy still, after all, but Jacob knew that they were vulnerable here the longer they stayed in the house. The longer he had to pay attention to George instead of whatever the outlaw was doing.

"Okay," he said as he finished. "That should keep you set until someone else can take a closer look. Now, you have to stay put, George Thatcher. Promise me you will wait here for me to bring your family to you."

"But, how can I?" he wailed. "I can't just sit here."

"You must. You will be no good to anyone if you get in the way out there. Am I understood?"

"Yes. I know. You're right. I promise."

"And when your family all come back in here, you'll be here to welcome them."

"I suppose."

Jacob sighed. That had to be good enough. He couldn't afford to waste any more time reasoning with a teenage boy. He thought back to the way he had been at that age, the way his brother Jackson had tried to get him to do things. This had to be good enough.

"You keep the rifle," he said. "Just in case. You never know when a fight may find you."

George nodded, and sat up a little straighter, his hands ready on the gun.

"The next time you see me, it will be with your family."

Without any sentimental good-bye, Jacob trudged through the house back to the front door. This time he didn't just walk out. He peered through the doorway toward the barn, toward where Maloney was likely still holed up with the three girls and the parents.

Jacob's luck held—the barn door was still closed tight with a small halo of light shining through the planks. He could hear muffled yelling and thumps coming from within the structure. The outlaw must still be in there. All Jacob had to do was get in there as well and disarm the man. Maloney was trying to keep five people under control with just himself. There would be a weakness there, and Jacob would find it.

His path to the barn door was direct, no obstacles, nothing to watch out for other than Maloney shooting at him again, and that had already happened twice now. He could handle it. Jacob's plan was just to go for it. Straight in. He was tired of chasing, tired of trying to give each outlaw a chance to come quietly.

Jacob could overpower the outlaw both physically and with firepower. It was time for him to use his leverage and his competence instead of continuing to give the man chance after chance.

He ran as quickly as he could to the barn, pausing outside the door to listen. One of the girls was sobbing. A gagged man's voice tried to protest, but Jacob couldn't make out any words.

"If you don't stop it like I've told you, I'll take that pretty little girl of yours and—"

That was it. That was enough. Jacob threw open the barn door, stepped inside, and trained his weapon on the outlaw.

"Stop, Maloney. You are under arrest."

The other man spun around and glared at Jacob. He aimed his own weapon back at the bounty hunter, but held his fire. In the brief moment Jacob had to take stock of the situation, he noticed several things.

In the time it had taken Jacob to bandage up George's arm and return to the barn, Maloney had somehow managed to tie up all three girls again. Jacob's heart sank. He had hoped the three would be angry and scared enough to avoid being captured again. Hoped all three of them together would be enough to keep Maloney from gaining the upper hand.

The parents were also tied up. All five of the family members sat on the ground against the far wall, tied up and gagged, almost exactly as Jacob had found them not an hour earlier. It was as though he was going backward. No progress had been made. Nothing had changed. He was right where he started.

But as he looked closer, he realized that Sarah, the middle girl, was clutching her leg. A small puddle of blood had gathered in the dirt underneath her, and both of her hands tied in front of her were dark red from the wound. Eliza sat next to her, leaning close to her sister, but with her own hands bound couldn't do any more to comfort her sister.

Jacob felt a wave of fury course through him.

Seamus Maloney had shot a child. A ten-year-old girl.

Jacob's anger was almost palpable. This could not stand. This man would not get away with such brutality.

"Seamus Maloney, you are under arrest," he said again.

Maloney froze where he stood but did not back down.

CHAPTER FOURTEEN

Jacob and Maloney stood only a few yards apart inside the barn. Neither man fired, but both had guns pointed at each other while most of the Thatcher family looked on. The barn was lit by a single lamp, dirty globe blocking much of the light. It had been set carelessly on the dirt floor near a bale of hay. One wrong move, one foot accidentally tripping and the lamp could get knocked over and the entire structure sent up in flames.

The arrogance of this man—of every outlaw Jacob had gone after—never ceased to amaze him. They all seemed to believe they were invincible, that somehow they were the special ones. They believed that any mistake they made was someone else's fault. Every outlaw acted as though the whole world was against him and he was only taking his due.

And it was Jacob's job to teach them otherwise. They should feel fortunate that he was only in charge of bringing them in to meet the law. If he was in charge of the punishments for the litany of cruelties they would be sorry.

But now. Here at the Thatcher family ranch, Jacob finally had this outlaw in his sights. Now the outlaw was the one who was stuck. Maloney couldn't shoot and run like he had back in Haven. He couldn't victimize any more children. He couldn't murder and steal just for his own gain. The bounty hunter would be bringing him in.

"Your murdering days are over, Maloney," Jacob said. "I will not stand by while you harm this family any further."

Maloney laughed, a hard, cold laugh that revealed the deep cynicism in the man. "Who the hell are you?"

"Jacob Payne, bounty hunter."

"Oh, well well well. You must think you're something special to follow me all the way out here. It was you I shot back in town this morning, wasn't it?"

Jacob declined to respond, but continued to keep his gun trained on Maloney.

"You think you can best me?" the outlaw said. "You're not even walking away from here alive, let alone with me in your custody. This all ends for you here."

"Do I think I can best a man who felt he needed to shoot a child to prove his strength?" Jacob said with a scoff. "Yeah. I do."

Jacob was seething. He had never before taunted an outlaw like this. But, to be fair, he had never before had to deal with a piece of scum like this.

Maloney narrowed his eyes and gritted his teeth. "You don't know nothing."

"I know that only a coward would steal money rather than work for it."

"What did you say?"

"Only a coward would have to be on the run."

"I'm not a coward," he said coldly.

"What else would you call a man who murders seven people, including women? What else would you call a man who imprisons an entire family, including young girls?"

"Shut up."

"You need to overpower the weak and defenseless in order to make yourself feel big."

"You shut your mouth!"

"Only a coward would shoot at the law while

he ran away," Jacob said bitterly, gesturing to the wound in his abdomen.

"I said shut it!"

"Only a coward would shoot *a child*."

"Goddamn it—" Maloney came barreling at Jacob, dropping his gun to his side and shoving the man. "I'm not a coward, you motherf—"

"Prove it," Jacob said, interrupting him and shoving him back. "Just you and me."

"I'll kill you."

"Maybe. But if you do, at least you'll know it was a fair fight, and you didn't hurt the defenseless. It would be the first time in your life you actually earned what you took."

"A fair fight?" Maloney laughed. "A fair fight from a man who kills for money? No bounty hunter has ever given a fair fight."

"I've never killed anyone that didn't shoot at me first," Jacob said quietly. "If you'd like to just turn yourself in, I'm happy to take you back to Tucson alive and you don't have to risk it."

"And give you another reason to call me a coward? I don't think so."

"A duel then."

"What?"

"That's your other choice. Turn yourself in to me. Let me take you in safely and easily and let the law in Tucson deal with you. Or a duel and you can try to prove you're as much of a man as you seem to think you are."

"Right now?"

"Yep. Quick draw," Jacob said. "If you're as big as you think, you should have no trouble getting rid of me."

He could see the outlaw was getting angrier and the implications that he was a coward, that he wasn't capable of dispatching with the bounty hunter.

"You got it, boyo," Maloney said.

The flash of fury in his eyes worried Jacob, but he knew he was quick enough with his gun that he stood a chance. It was either this, or put the safety of the Thatcher family at risk, while Jacob tried to overpower him here. Near the flame. Near the children.

No, far better to only put himself at risk in a task of skill.

Jacob was worried, but not enough to go through the alternative.

"Outside then," he said.

It infuriated Jacob to have to leave the family tied up like this, but it was for the best. He couldn't trust the outlaw for a split second. This was a smaller evil he would have to put up with to defeat the larger evil of the man himself.

Instead, Jacob met Mr. Thatcher's eyes. "I'll be back. As soon as this is dealt with I'll come back and free you. I just need y'all to stay calm. Trust me."

The man nodded, his wife sniffed back a tear. Jacob took a deep breath and turned the whole of his attention back to Maloney.

Jacob picked up the lamp himself, bending down without taking his eyes off of Maloney. He backed out of the barn door, lamp held in front of him with one hand, with the gun in the other.

"Twenty paces," Maloney said. "Then you die."

"Twenty paces," Jacob agreed. "Then we'll see."

The expanse of dirt between the barn and the home was plenty big enough to hold their duel. Keeping his eye on the outlaw, Jacob walked to roughly the center and set the lamp down. That single point of light would be between them. Neither man would have better light or a better chance to aim than the other. Jacob knew the only reason Maloney was agreeing to any of this was to prove he wasn't a coward, so weighting the circumstances in either direction would get a protestation.

Both men were loath to turn their backs on the other.

"Holster your gun," Jacob said.

"You first," Maloney countered.

Jacob shook his head, but returned the revolver to his hip. A quick draw duel required the gun being drawn after all. Maloney, for his part, did the same. Jacob held his breath the entire several seconds until the outlaw's hand was off of his gun. Both men walked their twenty paces away from each other before facing off again.

Jacob waited. He let his eyes adjust to the dim light. It was now well after sunset, and they only had the small lamp between them to illuminate. He could see well enough to make out Maloney's shape. That's all he needed. The color of his shirt or the sweep of his mustache was unimportant in a situation like this.

He could make out some of Maloney's movements. The darkness, the shadows, it all played tricks on his eyes. And still he waited. He would not be the first to shoot.

Jacob heard the swish of gun being pulled out of leather, he heard click of Maloney's gun firing. Without even giving himself time to think, Jacob fired in return.

He braced himself for another bullet wound, but none came.

Instead, he saw the faint outline of Seamus Maloney collapse into the dirt.

Jacob froze momentarily. Though he knew he was a good shot, he hadn't for a second believed he was invincible. The fact that he had felled Maloney and yet not gotten hit himself was shocking enough to give him pause. Of course, Jacob reminded himself with a hand to his abdomen. He had already been shot earlier that day.

He cautiously walked the several yards to where Maloney was in the dirt. The outlaw writhed only a little. When Jacob was standing over him, the other man looked up.

"I'm not a coward," he said weakly.

The pool of blood around the outlaw's body spread rapidly. The last breath left his body and his head dropped to one side.

It was done.

For the first time since he came to the west, Jacob had killed a man while trying to bring him to justice. Now he was what he had always guarded against. He was a man who killed for money.

Jacob crouched down in the dirt and with one hand closed the eyes of the deceased.

CHAPTER FIFTEEN

Once Jacob had untied the Thatcher family, seen to the wounds of the children and to the handling of Maloney's body, he didn't have any energy to go back to town that night. Mrs. Thatcher insisted that he stay the night and he had no objection. He had promised himself a rest, after all, and tonight was a good time to start.

The body of Seamus Maloney was bundled up in a homespun tarp that the Thatchers had on hand. When Jacob had protested using their property, Mrs. Thatcher scolded him.

"We could very well be gone and never use this again if it weren't for you, Mr. Payne. This piece of cloth is replaceable. Please let us give this to you. Let us help in this small way."

Jacob had let her, and Mr. Thatcher had helped him roll the body in the cloth, and place it in the far corner of the barn.

Jacob had gratefully accepted a full dinner from Mrs. Thatcher, as well as the cot in the pantry from George. Given his fitful night of rest the night before, and the exertions of the day, it's no wonder that Jacob slept soundly well after sunrise.

But he didn't stay long. The bounty hunter needed to get back to Tucson and deal with the repercussions of the outlaw's capture. The next morning, Thatcher helped Jacob place the corpse over the saddle of Maloney's horse, securing it tightly for the transport back into the city. Jacob said good-bye to the family, making special care to praise George for his actions and make sure the girls were all right after the trauma they had suffered.

The ride back to Tucson felt much longer than the ride to Haven had. The horse following with the body draped over it seemed to stay in his mind despite the fact that he never looked at it.

He had been so proud of his record of never having killed a man while seeking a bounty, but now he could no longer say that. Of course,

Jacob knew his actions were wholly defensible. It had been a fair duel and Maloney had been given every chance, more than once. But this was a line that could never be uncrossed.

Jacob and Blaze arrived in Tucson just before noon and the hottest part of the day. He went straight to the coroner with Maloney's body. Jacob needed to take that step and begin to move past it. He could tell Santos about it later, and claim his reward.

Although Jacob didn't feel right about taking money for killing a man, he understood that sometimes this was part of the job. He wasn't sure how he would spend the rest of the day. Maybe have the doctor take a look at his wound. Maybe just go to the saloon for a drink. Whatever he did, Jacob hoped Santos didn't have any pressing jobs for him at that moment.

As Jacob was exiting the coroner's office, a familiar figure exited the storefront opposite.

The woman carried a basket full of onions that she was rummaging in as she walked not looking where she was going. Jacob hurried across the street to catch her before she stumbled right off the boardwalk.

"Be careful, miss," he said, quietly enough that only she could hear.

Bonnie Loft's face lit up with joy when she noticed who was offering her his hand.

"Why! Jacob! You're back, already?"

He nodded.

"What's wrong?"

She could sense a difference in him just in those few short seconds. Jacob smiled, grateful for her compassion and her attention.

"Oh, you know. Every case is hard in its own way. I'll be all right."

She smiled in return.

"It's good to see you," he continued.

"Thank you."

"I'd like to see you again."

"Again? Right now?"

"Are you on your way home? Let me walk you there."

She nodded demurely, and he took the basket from her. The walk to her boarding house wasn't long, certainly not enough for him to explain to her everything that had happened or what seeing her now had meant to him. All he could do was hope she was available for future plans. Tomorrow. And the day after that. And after that and after that forever.

"Well. Here we are," she said when they reached the building.

"Bonnie, I want to say something."

"Oh?"

He set the basket down at their feet and took both of her small hands in his.

"You've been the best part of my life here in Tucson."

"Oh . . . I . . ."

"Wait. Please. I need you to know what your friendship these last few months has meant to me. When I first arrived, I was angry and lost and probably sometimes took risks I shouldn't have. But now, with your compassion and attention, I find myself wanting to be a better person. Bonnie, if . . . if it's all right with you, I'd like to court you in earnest."

The smile that broke across her face could only be heartfelt and genuine. There was no faking a look like that. "I'm honored," she said.

Jacob took her in his arms for the first time. The way she fit against his body felt as though they had been made for each other.

Bonnie lifted her face to his. He took her cheek in one hand, with his other arm wrapped around her waist, leaned down, and kissed her softly on the lips.

When he pulled his face away, she was blushing.

"Jacob . . ."

"I know. I should have asked. But, Bonnie, I've been waiting to do that for weeks. Coming home after that trek, knowing you were here waiting for me is the best thing that has happened to me in a long time."

Download this story for free—http://
atbutler.com/jp-free

Lonesome Trail

Before Jacob Payne arrived in the Arizona Territory, before he was a bounty hunter, before he learned how to survive in the desert, he had to travel west. Innocents in trouble, quirky characters and life-threatening peril are along every mile as he

passed from Virginia through Texas to the desert of Arizona.

When Jacob comes across a family that has fallen victim to horse thieves, he can't just ride on and leave them to his fate. He's not yet a bounty hunter, but Jacob Payne can still hunt down the evil-doers. Tucson will be waiting for him once he brings these men to justice.

Sign-up to download this prequel story for free from my website: **http://atbutler.com/jp-free**

ALSO BY A.T. BUTLER

Jacob Payne, Bounty Hunter Series:

Trouble By Any Name

Danger in the Canyon

Justice for Jasper

Blood on the Mountain

Outlaw Country

Death By Grit

Desert Rage

Arizona Legacy

Fool's Demise

Silent Night

Courage on the Oregon Trail Series:

Westward Courage

Faithful Trail

Frontier Sisters

Unyielding Heart

Wild Promise

Fierce Dreams

Novels by A.T. Butler:

Hawke's Revenge

Loyalty's Price

——————

Desert Rage, book seven in the Jacob Payne series,
is now available!!

Someone is after Jacob.

When the Slippery Stone outlaw gang get caught up
in a bank robbery, Jacob realizes just capturing the
guilty parties won't be enough.

_If you love classic westerns full of romance and action,
you'll love Jacob Payne._

Get your copy now — http://atbutler.com/jp7

ABOUT THE AUTHOR

I grew up in the southwest—California Missions, snakes and constant threat of drought weaving the backdrop of my childhood.

But it wasn't until I moved to Texas a few years ago that the magic and mythology of the American West began to seep into my soul.

I'd love to write about Jacob Payne for a long time. ...

If you enjoyed this book, a review on your favorite retailer would be greatly appreciated.

Be sure to sign up for my newsletter for all the updates on future books.

- A

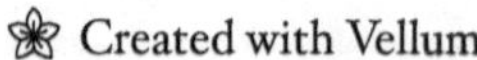 Created with Vellum